M. S. Power was born in Du
France. He has worked as a '
but now lives on the Oxfordshire/Buckinghamshire
first novel, HUNT FOR THE CLOWNS, was published to critical acclaim in 1983. His three novels comprising the children of the North trilogy, THE KILLING OF YESTERDAY'S CHILDREN, LONELY THE MAN WITHOUT HEROES and A DARKNESS IN THE EYE, were published in 1984, 1986 and 1987 respectively.

Also by M. S. Power in Abacus:

Lonely the Man Without Heroes
The Killing of Yesterday's Children
A Darkness in the Eye

BRIDIE AND THE SILVER LADY

M. S. Power

SPHERE BOOKS LTD

Published by the Penguin Group
27 Wrights Lane, London w8 5TZ, England
Viking Penguin Inc., 40 West 23rd Street, New York, New York 10010, USA
Penguin Books Australia Ltd, Ringwood, Victoria, Australia
Penguin Books Canada Ltd, 2801 John Street, Markham, Ontario, Canada L3R 1B4
Penguin Books (NZ) Ltd, 182–190 Wairau Road, Auckland 10, New Zealand

Penguin Books Ltd, Registered Offices: Harmondsworth, Middlesex, England

First published in Great Britain by William Heinemann Ltd 1988
Published in Abacus by Sphere Books Ltd 1989
1 3 5 7 9 10 8 6 4 2

Copyright © M. S. Power 1988
All rights reserved

Printed and bound in Great Britain by
Richard Clay Ltd, Bungay, Suffolk

Except in the United States of America,
this book is sold subject to the condition
that it shall not, by way of trade or otherwise,
be lent, re-sold, hired out, or otherwise circulated
without the publisher's prior consent in any form of
binding or cover other than that in which it is
published and without a similar condition
including this condition being imposed
on the subsequent purchaser

For
M. J. Cuddiford

. . . only against Death shall he call for aid in vain; but from baffling maladies he hath devised escape.

Sophocles: *Antigone*

· ONE ·

THEY PLANNED THE killings together, secretly. That is what Bridie tells the nice young doctor in the crisp white coat who questions her, watching him as he nods away as if really understanding and smelling not unpleasantly of medical concoctions that seem to have seeped into the pores of his skin. 'We planned them together in secret,' she says simply, smiling shyly as though bewildered by the fuss everyone is making.

'Why, Bridie? Can you tell me why you killed them?'

Bridie frowns, puzzled that such a question should be posed. She looks away for a moment, staring up at the ceiling, tracing the spidery patterns in the grey, cracked plaster, making them into rivers and hedgerows and low, stone walls where tiny, nervous animals dwell.

'Can you tell me why?' the doctor persists, brushing an invisible fleck of something from his baggy corduroy trouser leg, sounding overly casual.

Slowly Bridie lowers her head and gazes into his eyes, unblinking. They are pretty eyes, she decides: eyes that are capable of understanding suffering and joy, but mostly suffering.

'Can you tell me why?' the nice young doctor with the pretty, understanding eyes asks for the third time, patiently.

Bridie nods.

'Why?'

'Lady said it was the only thing to do.'

'Lady?'

Bridie nods again and leans forward. 'My Silver Lady,' she explains seriously. 'She was quite upset about it, though. She just couldn't see any other way out.'

'Silver Lady?' the nice doctor asks, sounding surprised for the first time, his eyes not so understanding now: suspicious.

'Yes.'

The woods did not cover a wide area. They stretched across one side of the narrow valley and moved some way up the hill beyond, stopping just before the summit as though resting, exhausted by the climb. At the foot of the hill where the ground was most fertile they grew high and straight and lush, their magnificent arched branches concealing the muddy, rutted track that gave reluctant, almost secretive, access to the village. Yet, despite the mystery and darkness that brooded within, there was nothing sinister or frightening about these woods, although some harassed parents did try to make them so, threatening recalcitrant children with reprisals of abominable ferocity to be wreaked by unearthly, marauding monsters which lurked, slavering, in the undergrowth. Old people, too, tended to give the woods an unwitting portentous awesomeness, saying that the massive oaks and elms and beeches and firs sent their spirits skywards in the winter, bleeding their leaves to set those spirits free: it was, they maintained, the sighing souls of the trees that one heard as their branches creaked and groaned in the winter gales. Some spoke of great birds that accompanied all souls to the feet of Christ; and on clear nights, made brittle by frost, the feathery tips of the giant pines looked, indeed, like monstrous winged creatures feeding on the stars.

It was, quite probably, these mythical inferences to some

tenuous and unfathomable link between birds and the spirit world that gave the old owl its ominous reputation. True, it was exceptionally large for a tawny, and its plumage had a rare, shimmering, silver tinge to it that made its passage eerily spectral. Although rarely seen, it had been known to leave cover and swoop down to carry off new-born lambs in March, but even this undoubted feat hardly merited the all but numinous powers attributed to it. It was as though (possibly because it was the only creature identifiable as living permanently in the woods) it was regarded as representing everything else that lived there, representing even the silently moving force of the trees.

Over the years the might and potency of the owl was embellished by superstition so that it no longer seemed prudent to dismiss as mere coincidence that someone always died in the village within days of the great bird being sighted beyond the boundaries of the wood; and no longer was it treated as imagination when its screeches were heard slicing through the darkness to mingle with the lamentations keened by the mourners on the nights before the funeral. Now, when someone reported seeing the owl, old people sucked in their breath and prayed a little faster, a little more fervently, wondering if their time had come. Doors were locked and curtains pulled tight to impede death's visitation, and in their minds those who considered themselves as unlikely victims sorted out their mourning clothes.

It was not altogether surprising, therefore, that when Ignatious Wyett saw what he swore was a human shape running into the woods he endowed the old owl with the power of transmogrification – 'slipping out of itself and into human shape,' he explained for the benefit of those who looked aghast at such a mighty mouthful of a word. And he found nothing incredible in this; nor, indeed, did anyone else he mentioned it to. They accepted the possibility in much the same way as they had been taught to accept God: a distinct if unproven virtuality, and certainly not something to be scoffed at or questioned.

From time to time, after Wyett's sighting, other people claimed to have seen the figure – always fleetingly, a wraithlike substance that moved with uncanny speed, never seeming to touch the ground, always sheering away from the observer, managing to suggest a sad preoccupation with searching for something irrevocably lost. In the end, so familiar did the tales of the creature's appearances become that the villagers settled it in their minds as part of their community. They left food for it at the edge of the woods each Friday, and they respected its clear desire for privacy, withdrawing immediately the food had been placed and never looking back. They graced the mournful creature with a further potency convincing themselves that, in its own mysterious and generous way, it protected the woods and kept what danger might be lurking there under firm control. Oddly, the menace so often ascribed to spirits was never exploited: they believed that to abuse its presence would incur its wrath, causing it to don its feathery guise and plummet down on them, perpetrating untold havoc in vengeance or, far worse, that it might abandon them altogether.

Sometimes, usually in winter and always on calm, windless days, an inexplicable flurry of air would blow from the woods and caress the valley, carrying the distinct sweet scent of lavender: people would smile knowingly when this happened, content in the knowledge that the spirit was still there watching over them; and, in the harsh, bitter months before spring, they did not begrudge the occasional lamb since, to their way of thinking, it meant their protector's belly would be filled, helping it survive that tricky time of year.

'Your Silver Lady?' the young doctor asks again, the erstwhile attitude of compassionate understanding freezing awkwardly on his lineless, chubby face.

'That's right,' Bridie agrees cheerfully, her eyes flicking about the room before coming to rest on the neat row of pens and pencils the doctor has clipped in the top pocket of his crisply starched white coat.

'And where does your Silver Lady live, Bridie?'

Bridie thinks deeply, furrowing her brow. 'Everywhere, I suppose,' she answers finally.

'Everywhere?'

'Yes,' Bridie affirms, sounding more confident.

'You mean like Jesus?' the doctor suggests, culling that divinity from some vaguely remembered precept in the catechism.

'Something like that. Only Lady's real.'

'I see,' the doctor says he sees, but sounds anything but convinced.

Bridie beams, delighted.

'How long have you known her?'

'Oh, ages and ages.'

'Where did you first meet her?'

Bridie gives a little shrug. 'I don't remember. Maybe in my room. Maybe somewhere else.'

'Has anyone else met her?'

'I don't know,' Bridie confesses. 'But I expect so.'

The nice young doctor with the chubby face clears his throat and leans back in his chair. Bridie leans back too, and takes to smiling again, wondering why it is that her smiles, so well intentioned, seem to disturb him and make a little nerve at the corner of one of his pretty eyes jump.

'Could you let me meet her?'

Bridie stops smiling abruptly. 'Only if she *wants* to meet you. She's *very* fussy about things like that. She always refused to meet Mummy.'

'But you might be able to arrange it?'

'I could try.'

'Where would we have to go?'

Bridie raises her eyebrows and gives a short, chiding laugh. 'Go? Nowhere, silly. Lady comes to me wherever I am.'

'You just call her and she comes?'

'I don't have to call her. She knows when I want her.'

'Don't you want her now?'

'Why?'

'Well, to help you?'

'Why should I want her to help me now?'

The doctor stands up and starts walking about the room, measuring his stride, thinking, using each step to underline each thought. Bridie watches him curiously.

Ignatious Wyett was peeved and upset when he heard the news and decided immediately to test the feelings of others, unwilling to find himself out on a limb. Standing in Mrs Canty's tiny shop, pretending to read the ingredients on a tin of custard powder, not even bothering to look up as he spoke: You'll have heard someone's bought the old mill? he asked nonchalantly.

Mrs Canty had, of course, heard: she heard everything; but she was certainly not about to admit as much, regarding all information transmitted across her counter as on a par with the sacred secrecy of the confessional. Indeed, widowed and childless, she had espoused silence with the fervour of nunnish celibacy, and while she revelled unrestrainedly in listening to gossip she never permitted herself to participate. So rigorous and unbending was her refusal to divulge confidences that it had become something of a village pastime to try and entrap her, even though all efforts so to do had thus far proved fruitless. Now, she tidied a pile of brown paper bags, and said nothing.

– Some woman, I understand, Mr Wyett went on regardless.

Mrs Canty waited.

– From the city. Coming to savour the delights and tranquillity of our rustic charm, no doubt. To survey the peasants at work and play.

Mrs Canty humphed.

– Children too, Ignatious added scathingly, making them sound like the ultimate catastrophe.

Mrs Canty looked up quickly: she had heard of only one child and was irked that any more might have slipped in without her knowledge. She covered her irritation with a short cough, and said: It'll be nice to have children running about the place again.

Ignatious Wyett eyed her balefully. Lovely, he agreed with

mountainous sarcasm. Just lovely.

– New blood is good blood, Mrs Canty observed.

– New blood is just plain bloody, Mrs Canty.

– You're a very cynical man, Mr Wyett.

Ignatious agreed willingly. True, he admitted. It's one of the few protections we mortals have left to us in this appalling world. The jaundiced eye, Mrs Canty. Best defence given to man. The jaundiced eye.

– Rubbish.

– Oh I think not, dear lady. Although I might have agreed with you once.

And there had been, indeed, a time when Ignatious Wyett had accepted life at face value, had embraced it and allowed it to suckle his pleasures. But such optimism had come to an abrupt halt, and Ignatious Wyett, orphan, prodigiously intelligent, actor *manqué*, whimsical evangelist, con-man (not only of others) and, for five glorious months, fire-eater and sword-swallower in Benny Cahill's Travelling Circus, was a disillusioned man, galled by the fact that he was forced to admit that his downfall, if such it could be called, was his own doing. The hand of God (or Orlac, as he sometimes despondently thought of it) had played no part. Or, if it had, it had belonged to some deity with a particularly warped sensitivity, some dismal god bent on harassment.

– Yes, he told Mrs Canty, I might have agreed with you once.

'What I'd like you to do, Bridie, if you will, is to start right at the beginning and tell me everything that happened. In your own words. Take your time and tell me everything. Will you do that?'

Bridie clasps her fingers together and makes a steeple. Here's the church and here's the steeple; open the doors and look at the people, she thinks, spreading her fingers.

'Will you?' the doctor with the neat row of pens and pencils in his top pocket asks again hopefully.

Bridie gazes at him.

'Will you try and tell me all that happened?'

Bridie suddenly makes up her mind. 'All right, doctor,' she tells him brightly.

The doctor sighs a grateful sigh and uncrosses his legs. 'Good. Thank you, Bridie,' he says politely.

'You're welcome,' Bridie says, remembering her manners too. Then: 'Can we start that tomorrow?'

'– ? Yes. Yes, of course. If that would be better for you.'

'Yes, it would.'

'Why tomorrow, Bridie?'

'It'll be much better tomorrow.'

The doctor nods. 'I see. And why is that?'

Bridie takes refuge under a smile. It is better to keep him waiting a bit longer, she decides. Never rush into anything. That's what the Silver Lady always advised. Never rush headlong into anything, she said, or you could live to regret it.

'What will be different about tomorrow?' the doctor now asks, trying to fathom Bridie's reasoning.

'It will be a different day, won't it?'

The doctor smiles tolerantly but only with his mouth.

'That is certainly true.'

'That's why,' Bridie says, and clamps her lips tight.

– Seen them yet? Ignatious Wyett wanted to know.

Mrs Canty preened the smile that crossed her face and fixed her spectacles more firmly on her nose. Oh, yes, she admitted, turning away, leaving Ignatious to stew in his curiosity.

– Well?

– Well what, Mr Wyett?

– What are they like, for heaven's sake? Ignatious demanded peevishly.

Mrs Canty took her time about answering, busying herself by rearranging her modest display of jams and marmalades, making the pots into a pyramid. In fact, she was not at all sure how best to respond: the baby boy had been hidden in his pram and she had only seen the little girl through the window as she waited outside, her nose pressed against the glass, her features thus distorted, and the mother, a pretty woman, certainly, if one liked those rather skinny, made-up city types, had been nervous and fidgety, acting like someone only comfortable when shopping in a crowd, and had said very little, but studied the price of each item carefully before purchasing it. Still, Mrs Canty's reputation demanded that she divulge something: They seem very nice, she said, deciding this was adequately charitable and non-committal.

– Nice! Ignatious scoffed. Nice, indeed! That tells me precisely nothing, Mrs Canty.

Mrs Canty finalised her arrangement and returned to the counter looking smug. What did you expect, Mr Wyett? she asked innocently. The child remained outside, and Mrs Lynch only wanted a few basics. *I* don't believe in judging what people are like after just a few seconds of conversation, she added, making of her righteousness a definite rebuke.

– An impression is all I ask for, Mrs Canty. Surely a lady of your perspicacity and vast wisdom formed an impression?

– Yes. Yes, I did that.

– Pray tell.

– Like I said: they seemed very nice.

Ignatious Wyett threw both his arms into the air in an exaggerated gesture of exasperation. You can be most vexing, Mrs Canty, he said. Most vexing. I see I shall have to find out for myself what these wretched people are like. But why you cannot give me an inkling as to what has descended upon us I cannot understand.

– I just told you what *I* thought, Mr Wyett, and I can't say any more than that. They seemed to me to be very nice although no doubt you'll be having your own ideas.

Ignatious grunted. No doubt. How did they get here?

– I'm sorry?

– How did they come? I haven't noticed a strange car.

– Oh. Brian Smith collected them at the station and brought them.

– Smith? Huh. He'll be no help. No help at all. Can't keep a thought in his head for more than a split second. Every day since September I've asked him to bring me a load of manure for my roses and he still hasn't done it. He probably didn't even notice they were strangers.

Mrs Canty relented a little. I can't tell you anything about the child, she confided, but Mrs Lynch struck me as a rather lonely woman who simply wants to be left alone.

– Oh, well that's fine. But will she and her miserable offspring leave us alone, I ask myself?

– You can ask yourself whatever you like, Mr Wyett. I should imagine she'll have far better things to be getting on with than to go about interfering with the likes of you.

– People don't have to *do* anything to interfere, Mrs Canty. There are people who can cause the most dreadful disruption by just being there.

– Yes, Mrs Canty said pointedly.

Mr Wyett ignored the jibe. Possibly he didn't even hear it. His eyes had suddenly become bright and darted about the shop. Yet he didn't appear to be looking for anything: he seemed, more, to be listening.

– Mr Wyett? Mrs Canty called.

Mr Wyett shook his head. I'm sorry. I was –. He shrugged.

– You looked most peculiar. Are you all right?

– Yes. Yes, thank you. I just had an odd feeling, he explained vaguely with a small shudder. A premonition, he elaborated. But of what I have no idea.

– You and your premonitions, Mrs Canty scoffed with a chuckle.

– Yes. Me and my premonitions.

– They'll be the death of you. That's what they'll be, Mrs Canty joked.

– I'm afraid you might be right, Mrs Canty. Very afraid you might be right, Mr Wyett said sadly, and walked out of the shop.

– Well, for God's sake, don't try using your damn premonitions as an excuse, Ignatious Wyett's counsel told him, thoroughly alarmed.

– It's the only excuse I have, Ignatious protested.

– I don't care what it is. You start on that tack with Judge

Corboy on the bench and he'll likely as not have you hanged.
– So what do I do?
– Plead guilty.
– But I'm not –
– You are, Ignatious. Okay, to your weird way of thinking, you're not. But you did get the money from those morons under false pretences.
– I told them what it was for.
– To help you rid the world of the devil.
– Yes.
– Great. Tell old Corboy that and see what happens.
– Won't he believe me?
– *I* don't believe you, and I'm your friend.
– *You* don't believe me?
– I believe that you believed that what you were doing was – had some reason behind it. That's why I'm trying to defend you. But you just persist with this daemonic banishment rubbish and I won't be able to help you. You could be committed as mad, you know. Please, just plead guilty to the fraud charge. You'll get a year. Two at the most. Then you can put this whole mess behind you.
– Mr Wyett! Mr Wyett! You've forgotten your butter, Mrs Canty called after him, shaking her head as she watched him continue to stride away from her.

'So, shall we make a start?' the doctor with the pretty, ever-changing eyes, who was his nice and friendly self this morning, asks.
'All right,' Bridie agrees cheerfully, eyeing the doctor: he hasn't put on his white coat and looks very unmedical in his colourful Fair Isle pullover: more kindly. He has his writing-pad on his knee and one of those ball-point pens in his hand, poised to write down everything she says.
'Would it be better if I asked you a few questions first – just to help you get started?'
'If you like,' Bridie says, wanting to oblige.

'It's whatever *you* like, Bridie. I don't want you to agree to anything that doesn't please you.'

'Thank you. Yes. You ask me some questions,' Bridie says, pleased that the doctor has swung things the way she wanted them of his own accord.

And the doctor smiles, believing he has just got his own way. 'Right,' he says confidently, and shifts to a more comfortable position on his wooden chair. 'How long have you lived at the mill in the village?'

Bridie starts to count on her fingers. (Bridie Lynch, the teacher called from her raised perch in front of the blackboard, her cold, addery eyes imitating her scathing voice as she pushed her rimless spectacles back on to the bridge of her nose with one thin finger. Bridie Lynch will you kindly stop that stupid habit of counting on your fingers? You're quite old enough to do simple addition in your head. Really! And Bridie turned scarlet and plotted horrendous reprisals on the girls behind her who giggled.) 'Eleven months and a bit,' she answers eventually. 'Just about a year,' she adds to tidy things up.

'Did you like it there?'

'Oh yes. Very much.'

'You were quite happy?'

'Yes. Quite.'

The doctor smiles. 'Does that mean quite or very?'

Bridie returns his smile. 'Very.'

'You liked it better than living in the city?'

'Lots better. The city was awful.' Bridie pauses and frowns. 'Of course,' she continues after a moment, 'I didn't *know* the city was so awful when I lived there because I didn't know what the country was like then.'

The doctor gives her an admiring look and nods slowly, dropping morsels of praise into the action, giving Bridie the impression that he regards what she has just said as quite profound or in some way significant. 'Did your mother think the city was awful too?'

Bridie gives an enormous shrug. 'I don't know. She never said anything about it.'

'Do you know why she decided to move to the country?'

'Of course I know,' Bridie says in a tone that implies she thinks the question stupid.

'And why was that?'

Bridie says nothing.

'Won't you tell me why?'

'You know already.'

'I'd still like you to tell me if you will.'

'The house we lived in was much too big and far too expensive to run. The oil it used for the central heating was perfectly ridiculous,' Bridie informs him, sounding very grown-up.

'I'm sure. No other reason?'

'Not that I can think of.'

The doctor eyes her quizzically. 'Your Daddy left you, didn't he?'

'He left Mummy. Not me.'

'Didn't he leave you too?'

Bridie gives a tight, dismissive laugh. 'Of course not. He left Mummy.'

The doctor accepts this and nods, and makes more notes on his pad, underlining a couple of words. When he is finished, he looks up and asks: 'Tell me how you spent your time, will you?'

'My time?'

'Yes. What you did during the day. What friends you had.'

'Where? In the city?'

'No, Bridie. In the country. After you moved.' The doctor seems a bit rattled.

'Oh,' Bridie says, pretending not to notice his discomfort but smiling inside.

'Go back to when you first arrived in the village. It might help you if you closed your eyes. Just try and see yourself – how did you travel to the village?'

'By train. Then someone met us at the station. Mr Smith. He took us the rest of the way in his old car.'

'Well, close your eyes and try and see yourself getting out of the car. You've come all that long journey in the train, and then you step out of the car. What was your first impression?'

Bridie does as she is told. She closes her eyes and leans back in her chair, filling her mind with the landscape she has created over the days on the ceiling. Her first impression? With her head thrown well back so the doctor cannot see, she peeps through her lashes and follows the crack that leads from the ornate rose in the centre of the ceiling. It goes outwards to a point over the window, winding across the plaster, higgledy-piggledy, and pretty, like the shiny trail some small insects leave in their wake, glittery threads strung along their path so they can follow them home again and not get lost.

'Do you remember?' the doctor asks.

Bridie sits upright again, blinking, pretending she has just opened her eyes, pretending, too, that she has been concentrating hard. 'Not exactly,' she lies.

'Nothing?'

'Nothing, I'm afraid.'

Bridie walked down the track, taking her time, placing her feet carefully to avoid stumbling in the ruts, her city shoes already pinching, the shiny patent leather of the toe-caps already scuffed and gashed. Every few strides she glanced at the woods either side of her, but only from the corners of her eyes as if pretending she was paying them no heed; as if, too, they held no fear for her. In fact they frightened her terribly: the unfamiliarity of such potent strength filling her with awe. She was just eleven, tall and gangly, and at that demoralising, awkward physical stage when nature seemed to be fighting a losing battle in its attempt to determine, once and for all, what ultimate and precise dimension her body should take. Her face was narrow and unpretty, and her unruly mop of blue-black hair made her appear paler than she actually was. There was no doubt that it was her eyes that made the biggest impact and saved her from being ugly: huge and round and darkest green (like fabulous emeralds, Daddy had once called them) but even when she smiled (as she often does, and often, also, for no apparent reason) her eyes withdrew from all participation.

At the point where the stream sneaked from the woods and trickled under the hump in the track she stopped, one foot slightly raised like a setter, and sniffed the air, her nostrils twitching. It was all so very new to her: the quiet was new: that throbbing, humming silence that falling leaves and small animals, tumbling water and small insects make. The smells were new. The colours, the texture of the air, the shapes created by the shifting clouds and shadows were all new. Ever since Brian Smith had met them at the station and transported them to the village in his rusting, protesting old Ford Zephyr, Bridie had been wonder-eyed and amazed that such a place so different to anything she had known should exist. At no time did she feel out of place or abandoned: from the moment she stepped from the car, the woods and the hills and the quiet had wrapped themselves round her, welcoming her, promising her comfort and understanding. It was as though whatever god had ordained her placement in a city had finally admitted the error of his ways and set about rectifying matters, albeit in a circuitous, cruel way.

– I'm afraid it is time, Mrs Lynch, that you face up to the fact that he's not coming back to you, Mr Gavin Lloyd, the solicitor (tall and gaunt and mournful as an undertaker) told Mummy when they were sure Bridie was out of earshot.

– I've already accepted that, Mummy snapped.

– Have you? Mr Lloyd sounded sceptical but equally concerned.

– Yes. Mummy could be very stern.

– Good.

– I've also decided to take your advice and sell the house.

Mr Lloyd beamed. Excellent, he enthused in the manner of a man permanently worried that his judicious, considered advice would not be taken.

– I've already started looking for something smaller.

– Excellent, the solicitor said again.

– In the country, Mummy added in a funny voice as though she had purposely been saving this up as a surprise.

– Ah, Mr Lloyd sighed, sounding taken aback, suggesting

with his timid exclamation that all things pastoral posed legalities he would much rather not be involved in.

– I should have enough left over from the sale of this to buy something more practical.

– Indeed you should.

– And I think we can manage nicely if I'm careful and we live quietly.

– Indeed. Mr Lloyd's head bobbed away as he agreed. And perhaps the country *is* a good idea. It will be better for the little girl to get away. She could be horribly teased at school. Children can be so cruel in times of stress. To each other, I mean.

– She's eleven, Mummy pointed out for some reason.

Mr Lloyd looked puzzled for a moment until it dawned on him what Mummy meant. Ah yes, he said. They do grow up so quickly now, don't they. In my day eleven was still very young.

– Yes, Mummy said, sounding a bit sorry.

– Tell me – how does she feel – about the, eh . . . the separation?

Mummy hesitated. I don't honestly know, she confessed quietly, her voice tinged with guilt. I really don't know. She never mentions her father now.

– She's getting over it then, Mr Lloyd decided, suddenly becoming expert in such matters.

– Perhaps she is.

– And the baby? How does she feel about the baby? Young Oliver?

– Why, she loves him. Absolutely adores him.

– Good. Good. I only ask because I have known cases of a terrible jealousy creeping in. Especially when – as in your case now – there is only one parent.

– Yes. No. Bridie's fine. I *was* worried when she suddenly stopped asking about her father. I thought – well, I thought she might be brooding.

Mr Lloyd chuckled kindly. Children get over heartbreak so very quickly. They forget, he explained. I'm afraid we adults tend to make far too much of the supposed scars of childhood.

He chuckled again. Making them an excuse for our own inadequacies, I suspect. In their funny way, children are not unlike animals: they know instinctively that the important thing is to get on with the business of living.

– I hope you're right, Mr Lloyd.

– I'm sure I am, Mr Lloyd was sure, and he stressed his surety by leaning forward and patting Mummy's hand.

– I hope so, Mummy repeated, while on the stairs, warm and snug in her woolly dressing-gown, Bridie hugged herself and smiled.

. . . Remembering that smile, Bridie smiled again. She spotted a large, flat, granite stone by the stream and settled herself on it, hugging her knees to her chest, her fingers interlocked about them. For several minutes she sat motionless, staring at the sparkling water, perhaps seeing the tiny fragments of primeval debris floating by, perhaps not. Then she unwound herself and reached out, gathering a handful of pebbles and tossing them, one by one, into the stream, aiming carefully at the centre of the circle made by each preceding stone. The plop, plop, plop reminded her of something, but of something she could not for the moment recall: like so many things, the sound seemed to belong to the night, to have been salvaged from a sparse, fragmented dream – a dream almost remembered but not quite, recognised only by its shadowy outline, the details blurred and misshapen. It was like, she thought, like staring into the woods that now surrounded her, trying to see through the gloom and into the very heart, and catching glimpses of fantasies and wonderful images until the boughs moved in the breeze, swaying almost mischievously, making the sunlight swerve and manoeuvre its way to the ground from another direction, each time highlighting a different aspect, making the heart of the wood move closer, then further away, then back again, constantly shifting, always tempting, seducing, calling.

– Your Dad's run off and left you, Patricia Brazier told Bridie bluntly in the school playground, at the same time offering her a piece of chocolate.

– No, he has not, Bridie said defiantly.
– Yes, he has. I heard my Dad say so last night. He must really have hated you and your Mum to just walk out and leave you both like that.
– You're lying, Patricia Brazier, Bridie shouted, furious at the burning tears that came to her eyes. You're always lying about things. You're the biggest liar in the whole wide world.
– No, I'm not, Patricia Brazier protested. Anyway, I wouldn't lie about something as awful as this. It's so shameful and humiliating, she concluded, stressing the final words since she liked the sound of them and had only learned them last night while eavesdropping on her parents.
– Yes, you would. You'd lie about anything just to make yourself sound important.
– I wouldn't. Really I wouldn't, Bridie. Not to you anyway. You're my best friend. Is it true he did things to you?
Bridie tossed the last pebble into the stream and stood up, stretching herself luxuriously as a cat. Then she shivered: it seemed to have become suddenly and unexpectedly chilly. Somewhere deep in the woods a dead, sapless branch fell to the ground with an echoing crash, frightening her.
– Mummy, where's Daddy? Bridie wanted to know, the moment she got home from school, standing across the kitchen from her mother, literally trembling in fear of the answer, looking vulnerable and very young in her convent-school uniform of practical grey.
For a moment Mummy seemed hurt, even distressed. Then she became angry, her face reddening the way it usually did after an argument, her lips tightening and becoming a thin, defiant line. He's away, she said finally, turning back to the sink and holding her fingertips under the tap, feeling for the water to run hot.
– For how long?
– I don't know, Bridie.
– For ever?
Mummy gazed out of the window. Maybe. I don't know.
– Have you explained the situation to Bridie? Granny

wanted to know, later that evening or perhaps a few evenings later but certainly at an hour when Bridie was supposedly tucked up tight and snug in bed under the blue-and-pink-and-yellow patchwork quilt that Daddy had found at an auction and produced with a magician's flourish, tossing it into the air so that it floated down over her like a lovely, soft, warm cloud that sparkled with colours like the ones you see in sunlight. It'll bring the colours to your dreams, Daddy explained, and he was always right.

– Not yet, Mummy told Granny.

– Why not, for heaven's sake?

– I don't know how.

– Just tell her, Granny ordered practically, her tone making it clear she had no time for unnecessary pussyfooting. A tough, crabbed old woman who still suspected her daughter's unexpected beauty as something that she would have to pay for eventually, she saw no point in wasting what time she had left and was not about to allow her daughter that luxury. That child of yours is quite bright enough to appreciate the problem, she said firmly.

– I know she is, Mummy replied, snapping the words off crisply.

– Well, tell her then and be done with it.

– All right. Mummy almost screamed that.

. . . Bridie lowered her arms only when they ached, and studied the watch one of Daddy's business friends had given her for Christmas. It was ten minutes to five and already a dusky gloom was setting in. She started to walk slowly back down the rutted track towards the village, wondering what sort of mood Mummy would be in: she'd been a bit strange since the move, sometimes not speaking for hours, sometimes talking a lot as though she had piled up the words during her silence and was letting them gush out in one torrent. Suddenly Bridie stopped and looked back the way she had come, sensing she was being watched. She saw nothing strange, and wondered if the trees could see and were watching her guardedly, perhaps upset by her intrusion. Then she smiled to herself and gave a little wave. It's only me, she said aloud, and listened as the words were grabbed by the echo and shaken through the trees. Only me, she repeated, quietly this time, and sadly. And it was as though whatever had been observing her was appeased, relaxed and accepted her presence as something not to be feared.

– Bridie! Mummy called, just after they had returned home from Sunday Mass. Come here a minute, will you? she requested, using that subdued, polite voice she always adopted after she had been praying, as if God might still be privy to her conversations and become peeved if she sounded strident. I want to talk to you.

Bridie came into the sitting-room (don't call it the lounge, darling. It's so vulgar. It makes your home sound like a cheap hotel) and stood just inside the door, still with her small white prayer-book in her hands, her fingers tracing the embossed gold crucifix, and stared at her mother who sat demurely on the edge of the armchair, clasping and unclasping her hands on her lap, the rings on her fingers making tiny, metallic clicks, like knitting-needles. Yes, Mummy?

– It's about – about Daddy.

Bridie said nothing. She continued to stare at her mother, determinedly keeping her expression bland and unhelpful.

– He won't be coming back to us, Mummy announced abruptly, taking the bull by the horns as Granny might say, sounding bitter: her hands worked overtime.

Bridie put her head on one side and pursed her lips. Is he dead? she asked in a tolerant, matter-of-fact way, aware that her mother's phrase was the standard method of explaining death to children who were supposed to find such things unbearable. Mummy looked shocked. No. Of course not. Of course he's not dead. He's just gone away and won't be back.

– Why?

That gave Mummy something to think about. Bridie watched her as she desperately searched her mind for an adequate answer, her eyes fixed on her daughter's face, almost pleading to be released from the obligation to reply. But Bridie was having none of that; nor was she about to be generous. Why? she asked again, sounding forcedly reasonable.

– I . . . He . . . Mummy floundered to a halt and looked away biting her lower lip.

– Did he hate us?

Mummy latched on to that in a hurry, the awfulness of the question perversely appearing as a bright ray of hope. No, he didn't hate us, darling. Not you anyway, nor Oliver.

Apparently satisfied, Bridie turned as if to leave the room. Then, pausing in the doorway, she gave her mother a long, curious smile. I *know* he didn't hate me, she said, and walked out.

Hours later Mummy was still sitting in the armchair: it sounded like she was sobbing.

– Oh dear, oh dear, oh me, Daddy was saying in that silly, paternalistic voice he affected when he felt Bridie wouldn't understand him if he spoke naturally. Has my little girl hurt herself? Here, let Daddy have a look. Why, it's only a little cut. I'll give it a big kiss and make it better. Which he did, kissing her grazed knee and cuddling her tight, his strong, comforting arms moving over her body, making her feel warm and wanted and loved, his breathing a series of low sighs. He jumped to his feet when he heard Mummy coming down the hall, the flip-flopping of her slippers making it sound like two people.

– What happened to your knee, Bridie? she asked, not too concerned.

– I fell and cut it.

– You better run upstairs and put some iodine on it.

– It's all right now. Daddy kissed it and made it better.

– Oh did he?

Bridie nodded.

– How kind of him, Mummy said but with a funny look, and immediately Daddy said he had to go out again, and left the house quickly.

Mummy spent a long time staring at the chair he had vacated, chewing her lips and constantly changing her expression as if she was arguing with herself. And she was in a bad temper all that evening; and later, much later when she would normally have been in bed, Bridie heard her talking to someone on the telephone, saying that she simply could not tolerate something a day longer.

And, in truth, Kathleen Lynch had, as she saw it, been pushed to the limit of tolerance, that limit proscribed and curtailed by both her frustration and her innate, Catholic incapacity to comprehend anything that strayed, however mildly, from what she believed to be strictly normal. Worse still, she had long since succumbed to the peculiar stringencies of Catholic wifery, and perversely blamed herself for her husband's problem – filching that euphemism from her mother who used it to embrace everything from the common cold to civil war. Indeed, it was her mother with her ramrod sense of female status who had first instilled in her mind the possibility that she was responsible.

– What are you talking about? her mother demanded, setting her face in the lines she adopted when settling down to solve a puzzle.

– You heard what I said, Kathleen told her, acutely embarrassed.

– Oh I heard what you said but I don't believe my ears.

– It's the truth.

– I simply can't understand –

– I didn't think you would, mother, Kathleen interrupted.

– I never heard such balderdash. Francis interfering with Bridie indeed! How could you even think such a thing. Look at the child. That's all you have to do. Does she look abused to you?

– For heaven's sake, mother, he doesn't hit her, or kick her, or put cigarettes out on her.

– Well, what *does* he do?

– He hugs her, and kisses her, and feels her, Kathleen said, and immediately wished she hadn't.

– That's what a father's supposed to do, Kathleen. You really are ridiculous. Bridie's a very lucky child to have a father who shows her such love and affection. I never got one ounce of either from my father, and you've said to me often enough that your Daddy, God rest his soul, never showed he loved you.

– Francis does it too much, Kathleen tried.

Her mother said nothing to that. She sat there, very upright as though tightly corseted, her thin-lipped mouth slightly open, silently incredulous.

– And when he kisses her it's on the mouth. Hard. Not just a peck, like a father – oh, I don't know.

– Have you said anything to Francis himself about it? her mother now wanted to know.

– Yes. No. I –

– It has to be one or the other, Kathleen, the old woman said, subtly using her daughter's indecision as a vague refutation of all she had said.

– I've tried. But he won't listen. He doesn't even deny it. He just walks away. *He* won't talk about it.

– I should think not too, her mother pointed out, typically dismissing any relevance her original question might have held. And I would say you're very lucky all he does is walk away.

– Christ, mother. I thought you'd help *me.*

– We can do without blasphemy, my girl. And I am trying to help you. You always do exaggerate things – even as a little girl you loved to exaggerate. Well, since you've asked me, I'll tell you what I think. I think you're just jealous.

– Jealous? Kathleen Lynch could hardly believe her ears. When her astonishment turned to pain she said, Jealous, again.

– It happens, her mother told her as though she knew about such things. A mother's role is often a lonely one, she added solemnly, endowing motherhood with passionate misery. It happens that some mothers become jealous of the affection their husbands show the children.

Kathleen shook her head in bewilderment. You really haven't understood one word of what I've been saying, have you, mother? Not a single word, she repeated sadly.

Her mother arched her neck. I am not a stupid woman, she

declared. I understand exactly what you've been saying and I think it's all very dirty and unworthy of any daughter of mine.

And perhaps it was in some forlorn effort to prove her point to her mother, albeit using a convoluted route, that Kathleen Lynch decided, once more, to try and talk the matter out with her husband. It took her several weeks to find the right time, finally broaching the subject one Sunday afternoon when Bridie was out at the zoo with Granny, and Francis seemed relaxed; and even then she was careful in determining the appropriate moment. It came when Francis tossed the newspaper to the floor and stretched. God, he said, it's the greatest pleasure in the world, Sunday, lazing in front of the fire.

Kathleen pounced. Francis, can we talk?

– Sure. What about?

– About us. About you. About you and Bridie.

The greatest pleasure in the world became, it seemed, the greatest burden. Francis Lynch froze, his arms coming to a halt half-way through their stretch and sticking out before him in an attitude of grotesque supplication. For Christ's sake, not that bloody crap again, he shouted, starting to get up.

– Please, Francis, don't – don't walk away from me this time. I'm trying to understand what is happening. I'm on *your* side. I'm not against you. I don't even blame you. I just want to talk it out so that we can do something about it.

– There's nothing happening, dammit. You've got this fucking idea in your head, and if I so much as look at Bridie – my own goddam daughter – you think I'm about to rape her. I don't do anything that any normal father wouldn't do.

– I can *see*, Kathleen screamed at him.

– Oh sure. Sure, sure. You can see. You can see what you want to see.

– I see you mauling my child, Kathleen said, spacing the words, giving them a venom far beyond her intention.

And perhaps it was this unexpected hatred that made Francis slump back in his chair. Immediately he rummaged in his mind for words that would precipitate his escape. The trouble was – and it was this which propounded the enormity of

Kathleen's insult, the trouble was that, no matter how he tried he could not suppress his feelings for Bridie. He loved her: but that, surely, was legitimate. And he loved to feel her soft, young, warm body close to him. The fact that he was aroused by such encounters, he argued, was normal. The trouble with you is that you're such a frigid, warped bitch that you can't stand to see me showing affection to Bridie the likes of which you're incapable of. He stood up and gave a hard, rasping laugh. You know what the real trouble is? You think *any* sort of love is dirty, that's your problem.

– Francis, please, Kathleen pleaded. You know that's not true.

– Oh no, you won't admit that, will you? You're so bloody busy cooking up accusations to sling at me that – oh, shit. I'm going out.

For the rest of the afternoon and into the evening Kathleen Lynch remained seated by the fire, hunched, her arms folded tightly across her breasts as though clasping something precious but fleeting to her heart, rocking herself from time to time. She looked, suddenly, very old, not in years but in that frightening, grey way that people do when subjected to lengthy isolation or peremptory loneliness. It was not until her mother brought Bridie home from her trip to the zoo that she shook herself back to awareness.

– You look dreadful, her mother observed. You should have come with us. We had a marvellous time, didn't we, Bridie?

Bridie nodded and studied Mummy's dreadfulness.

– I'm glad, Kathleen said.

– Where's Daddy? Bridie asked.

– He had to go out.

– Out? Granny asked. Out? On Sunday?

Kathleen nodded.

– Where to?

– He didn't say.

– Will he be back to tuck me in? was Bridie's immediate concern.

– I'm sure he will.

He wasn't, of course. Nor had he returned home by the time Granny decided it was time she left. What did you say to him this time that upset him so much? she asked, resetting her hat at a jaunty angle.

– Good night, mother.

– Just you watch yourself, my girl, mother went on, pulling on her gloves. (No woman is properly dressed without gloves, Kathleen.) If you're not careful you'll find yourself without a husband at all.

– Right now, nothing would suit me better.

– You're far too quick with the smart reply, Kathleen.

– Good night, mother, Kathleen said again, and shut the door without waiting for a reply.

The doctor nods and scribbles away, seeming to be enjoying himself, looking up only when Bridie stops talking. We are going to be good friends, he had told Bridie when they first met. We are going to get on like a house on fire. And that is what they are now doing: getting on like a house on fire. 'Do you think it might have been your Silver Lady who was watching you?' he asks after a pause, making that possibility sound plausible.

'No. I wouldn't think so. I don't think she knew about me then. It was only my first day, you see.'

'So it could have just been your imagination that someone was watching you as you walked home?'

'Oh yes,' Bridie agrees brightly.

'Just to go back a bit – you said the Silver Lady didn't know you then –'

'I wouldn't have thought so.'

'So when, do you think, did she get to know about you?'

Bridie frowns, and purses her lips. 'Soon after, I think. Yes, it must have been quite soon after because she came to see me a few nights later.'

That makes the doctor sit up and take notice. 'She came to see you a few nights later?' he asked, repeating Bridie's words in the way he always did when she caught him by surprise.

'Well, I'm not altogether certain it was her. I wouldn't swear to it or anything. But I *think* it was. I mean we didn't speak or touch each other, but I'm almost sure it was she who dropped in to have a look at me. Like I told you: she's very fussy who she speaks to. She was probably checking to make sure I was suitable.'

'But why do you think it was this lady who visited you?'

'I just got the feeling. She didn't actually come herself, of course. Not all of her anyway. She sent her shadow to have a peep.'

'Her shadow?' The doctor sounds interested in that, perhaps sniffing the tang of Jung.

Bridie nods. 'That's what she does, you know,' she explains.

'What?'

Bridie grimaces in annoyance, and copies from her memory the face of her schoolteacher. 'Sends her shadow to investigate first. It's how she protects herself. There's not much anyone can do to someone's shadow, is there? I think it's a very good idea, don't you?'

The doctor says he is sure it is. 'I'm sure it is,' he says.

'I thought you'd agree,' Bridie says, giving a little laugh before adding: 'I tried it myself once and it nearly worked.'

'Sent your shadow to –'

'Yes. Only into the next room to see if Mummy was asleep. Only I might have cheated.'

The doctor waits, raising his eyebrows by way of asking her to continue.

Bridie smiles shyly. 'Well, I think I *knew* Mummy was asleep before I asked my shadow to go in and look.'

'But your shadow went?'

'Oh yes.'

'And came back to tell you your mother was asleep?'

Bridie nods. 'But since I already knew Mummy was asleep it didn't count.'

'Didn't you ever try it again?'

'Not really,' Bridie says, but starts to twiddle her fingers like she often does when she lies.

'I would have,' the doctor says.

'I didn't need to,' Bridie tells him. 'I always had Lady to look for me.'

'Ah yes. So you did,' the doctor agrees and makes a note of that, stabbing the paper when he came to the full stop.

– My goodness, I thought you were lost, Mummy said in a jovial, good-natured way. What have you been up to?

– Walking. I went down to the river. Well, it's not a river really. A stream.

– Was it lovely?

Bridie nodded, picked up a slice of bread and butter from the table and started to munch. Very lovely.

– Oh good. You really are going to like it here, aren't you, darling?

– Yes. I'm sure I will.

– I'm so happy, Mummy said and sounded as if she meant it. You know what we're going to do? We're going to get to know each other. Really know each other like good friends.

– Yes, Bridie agreed, but without great enthusiasm.

– Now let's have tea and then early to bed with you. What we both need is a good night's sleep, then tomorrow you can explore some more while I unpack.

As it turned out, Bridie did not have a good night's sleep. She lay awake for hours listening to the unaccustomed stillness of the countryside; listening, too, to the conversation that had taken place several months ago when Daddy was still living with them.

– For God's sake, Francis, don't treat me like an idiot! Don't you think I know what's going on?

Daddy gave that cough he always gave when he was trying to think of something to say, to find a plausible excuse that would let his life proceed untrammelled; and there was the tinkling of glass as he made himself a drink. Daddy liked drink. More now than he used to. Although Bridie disliked the smell of alcohol on his breath the whisky did make him mellow and gentle: it was always after he had been drinking that he cuddled her most, holding her very tight in his arms, touching parts of her body that made her tingle all over, whispering to her. Poor Daddy, he seemed so *lonely*, so forlorn.

– It's got to stop once and for all, Mummy went on, almost shouting the word 'stop'.

– There's nothing going on, Daddy countered, the words resonant as if he had spoken directly into his glass.

– Oh, for Christ's sake. Why can't you just admit it? You must think I'm blind as well as stupid. I can see the way you maul the child. Your own child, dammit.

A long silence followed that, and Bridie, hunched in her favourite place at the top of the stairs (screened from view by the small, lattice-work gate that had been specially put there to prevent her falling down the stairs when she first began to walk), wondered why Mummy was being so angry and making such a fuss. She heard a glass being banged down heavily on the silver tray that held the drinks, and had just enough time to nip back into her own bedroom when Daddy slammed into the hall and thumped his way upstairs.

– That's right. Typical. Walk away from it, Mummy called after him from the foot of the stairs. The trouble with you Francis Lynch is that you won't face the truth and do something about it.

. . . Bridie must finally have dozed off since the next time she listened everything was quiet: not the brittle, expectant silence of temporarily suspended noise, but that cool, slumbering stillness that indicated a lengthy hush had been the order for some time. Then she remembered where she was, and smiled to herself. She lay on her back, the stiff, white, lightly starched sheets tucked in tight under the mattress, the multi-coloured quilt she had made certain to bring from the city (carrying it under her arm and stroking it fondly from time to time) pulled up under her chin. She listened wide-eyed to the crackles and groans of the old mill as it, too, settled down for a good night's sleep, its ancient timbers relaxing. Then, just as she had accustomed herself to these, the darkness was filled with calls and warnings, one possibly engendering the next. In the barn that backed on to their new garden, Michael Young's cattle shuffled their cloven hooves, and a few of them coughed irritating hayseeds from their lungs. In the shed next to them, the chickens clucked restlessly, some flying to a higher perch and showering those below with pellets of excrement, fluffing their feathers in mock defiance of whatever nocturnal spirits threatened before settling down on their haunches, their beady eyes nervous and alert, their combs flapping as they tossed their heads. Farther away, away across the still, frost-shimmering meadows, a lonely vixen threw back her mask and sent her chilling, sepulchral screams towards the moon, then screamed again and again as her cries went unanswered. Nearer, just outside Bridie's window, a family of hedgehogs gorged themselves, slurping their way noisily through the saucerful of bread-and-milk that Mummy had decided to leave out for them in a determined, premeditated gesture of conservation, her tentative step towards 'fitting in' as she put it, feeling an obligation to nourish the wildlife now that she had taken up residence in their midst. And that seemed overwhelmingly important to her all of a sudden: to fit in. She kept mentioning it as though she was making some last-ditch effort to locate that special place reserved for her on earth, as though, should she fail, she would be doomed to a state of perpetual melancholy. Strangely, she told Bridie she was 'feeding the night' although from what outlandish region of her mind she had hoisted that metaphor was anybody's guess.

Suddenly, without warning, something flew across the moon and dispatched its shadow through the window to inspect Bridie's bedroom. Then it flew back the way it had come, sheering away, signalling its passage with shrill, menacing screeches. When it had gone, the wind rose a little and blew for a few seconds, wiping every sound from the face of the night: everything was still and quiet again.

'You still haven't told me when it was you first actually saw your Silver Lady,' the doctor points out, doing his best to keep incredulity from his voice.

Bridie gives him a withering look. The silly man. He hasn't

been paying one scrap of attention. (Do pay attention, Bridie Lynch, the teacher snapped. I'm not just here as an ornament. It's quite pointless my trying to teach you anything if all you're going to do is stare out of the window and daydream. And it's not as if you can afford not to learn. Your test results were nothing short of a disgrace.) 'I didn't *see* her for ages,' Bridie explains with tolerant kindness. 'Nobody *sees* her for ages and ages,' she explains further. 'If she likes you, she'll *talk* to you, that's all. Then, when she's sure, she makes herself visible.'

'Oh, I'm sorry. I misunderstood,' the doctor apologises.

'That's all right,' Bridie forgives, feeling generous.

'Tell me, *how* does she speak to you, Bridie? I mean, if you don't see her –'

'From inside, of course,' Bridie interrupts, looking superior.

'So you don't actually *hear* her voice?'

'*I* do. I couldn't say for anyone else.'

Looking bewildered, the doctor decides to discontinue this line of questioning for the moment, and contents himself by making copious notes. 'Right,' he says finally, looking up and smiling pleasantly. 'When did she first speak to you from inside?'

'Oh, much later. After we'd lived in the mill at least three months. But she'd been watching me all the time, of course. Making up her mind, I suppose.'

'Do you remember exactly when you first heard her?'

Don't rush into anything, Bridie, or you'll live to regret it. 'Yes.'

'Will you tell me?'

Don't rush into anything, Bridie. 'Yes. But not today. I'll have to think about it very carefully. You wouldn't want me to make any stupid mistakes, would you?'

The doctor smiles. 'No. No, I wouldn't. Whenever you feel like telling me will be fine.'

'Yes,' Bridie says. 'I know it will.'

The doctor frowns at that and looks displeased; but he brightens again quickly as though trained to overcome setbacks and innuendos. He taps his ball-point pen against his teeth, mustering another question. 'How did you get on with the other people in the village?' he asks, changing tack. 'I mean, did you like them?'

Bridie shrugs. 'Some of them.'

'Some of them,' the doctor repeats and writes something down.

'Yes. Some of them,' Bridie offers, speaking slowly as though dictating.

'Who, for instance?'

Bridie sucks in her breath, holding it in her mouth, her cheeks bulging as she thinks. 'Mr Wyett,' she says after careful consideration, and eases the air from her lungs, now sucking in her cheeks and making her face gaunt. 'I liked Mr Wyett.'

'Mr Wyett,' the doctor says and writes the name down. 'He's nice is he? Tell me about him.'

Momentarily Bridie seems ill at ease. She shifts in her chair and looks down at her hands one of which strokes the other. 'There's nothing more to tell. I liked him, that's all,' she says, without looking up.

– So, you're the young lady who has come to join us in this rural backwater, eh?

Ignatious Wyett stood up from pruning his rose-bushes and lobbed the question over the prickly berberis hedge that designated his territory, grimacing a little as a twinge of lumbago stabbed him unexpectedly in the back, but managing to transform his expression of pain into something approximating a smile. Nearing sixty, he looked nowhere near that age, his narrow, rigid body giving the impression of a military background although nothing could have been further from the truth. Nevertheless, aware of this fraudulent image, he pandered to it, cultivating a moustache which he kept clipped in a thin, brigadierial line, and always striding rather than walking, his arms swinging as though on parade. There was even a precision about the way he did his hair, greasing it with a sticky pomade and combing it straight across the crown of his head, neatly covering the eroding baldness with uncharacteristic vanity.

– That's right, Bridie agreed pleasantly.

– And tell me – from your standpoint as a lady with obviously vast experience, Ignatious went on, moving from the rose-bed to the small wooden gate and waving his secateurs to embellish the vastness he referred to, tell me, what do you make of it?

Bridie grinned. I like it very much, she said.

– Do you now? Do you indeed?

– Yes, I do.

– Well, well. I cannot for the life of me see what charms this woebegone place could hold for a sophisticate like yourself.

Bridie grinned again, enjoying herself: although she could not put her finger on it there was something about this odd gentleman that charmed her: perhaps it was the fact that he was the first person in her experience who spoke to her as if she was an adult. There was nothing condescending about him, nothing patronising. And from time to time a little look crept into his eyes, a look she had noticed her father give which was comforting in its familiarity.

– Forgive me, he said now, removing one thick gardening-glove and holding out a bony hand. I've neglected to introduce myself. Wyett. Ignatious, Alexander, and, would you believe, Sebastopol Wyett.

– I'm Bridie. Bridie Lynch, Bridie told him, and shook hands.

– How do you do, Bridie Lynch.

– How do you do, Mr Ignatious Alexander Sebastopol Wyett.

And immediately they were both laughing: he uproariously, swaying back and forth, guffawing; Bridie discreetly, holding one hand over her mouth, tittering.

– Oh dear. Oh, deary me, Ignatious Wyett gasped. You know I haven't had a laugh like that since God knows when.

– Nor me, agreed Bridie. Wherever did you get a name like that, Mr Wyett?

– Foisted upon me, Mr Wyett said accusingly. Perhaps my addled parents thought life would not give me sufficient crosses to bear so they straddled me with one of their own devising.

How wrong they were, he added, suddenly serious. How very wrong they were! Still, he went on, cheering up a little, I've heard worse. Much worse. Well, perhaps not much worse, but worse nonetheless. So you like our rustic community?

– Yes. Very much. What I've seen of it.

– Good. Mr Wyett nodded approvingly. I'm pleased to hear it.

They stood in silence for a few moments looking at each other across the gate, Bridie smiling her enigmatic smile, an odd look, almost sensual, way beyond her years, filling her eyes, he just nodding his head as though to unbalance the sadness that Bridie's gaze sent looming into his mind.

– Well, I better get on with this pruning, he said at last. The surgery must be immediate or the patients will die, he added with a wry smile. Next time you pass you must come in for a visit, will you?

The look intensified, becoming curiously glazed. I'd like that, Mr Wyett. Thank you.

– Thank *you*, Bridie Lynch, Mr Wyett said, and turned away with odd abruptness.

– Thank you, Daniel, Mr Wyett said, shaking his counsel warmly by the hand.

– Wait until after the trial. You might not want to thank me then.

Mr Wyett gave a wry grin. That's why I am thanking you now.

– Tell me, Ignatious, as a friend – forget the legal claptrap – why did you do it?

Ignatious Wyett studied his friend's face, and was about to reply when Daniel Kelly asked: It wasn't really for the money, was it?

– No. No, it wasn't for the money. Mind you, that did come in pretty handy in those hard times, Ignatious said with a grin. You know, there is a sign outside a small menagerie in Valencay which has always touched me by its delicacy. It says: *On vous prie de ne pas vouloir inquiéter, effrayer, ni affoler les bêtes, qui ne sont là que pour vous faire plaisir.* That's what it was all about, my dear Daniel. *Pour faire plaisir*. Only it didn't quite work out like that, did it?

– I'm afraid not.

– Is it such a terrible place – prison?

– For some. But you're not there yet.

– No, not yet.

– There's always hope.

– Not always, Daniel. Not always.

'There must have been something special about him – Mr Wyett,' the doctor points out, checking the name in his notebook. 'You singled him out very quickly. What made him special?'

Bridie says nothing, but stares the doctor squarely in the eyes. Now, on the fourth day, she is getting bored with his questions, finding the whole thing no longer much of a game.

'If you had to name one thing about him that made you like him, what do you suppose it would be?' the doctor persists, getting to know Bridie's whims and peculiarities and believing her present silence is temporary.

But, for the first time since the start of the interrogation, Bridie looks truly angry. Her eyes adopt a curious blue sheen, and the right one seems to become suddenly lazy, remaining fixed on the doctor's face while the left one looks away. For the first time, too, she seems unsure of herself, becomes a child of uncertainty.

'There must be something you can put your finger on,' the doctor insists, pressing home what he hopes is an advantage: getting somewhere.

And Bridie surrenders. 'He told me stories,' she confides at last, but managing to make even this simple statement sound mysterious.

'Ah. Stories. About what?'

'All sorts of things.'

'For example?' the doctor asks, sounding a little tetchy, perhaps sensing the dissipation of his advantage: getting nowhere.

Bridie presents her most innocent smile. 'You know, doctor, just for the moment I cannot for the life of me remember,' she lies, looking deeply sincere.

– Well, this *is* a pleasant surprise, Ignatious Wyett enthused, and beamed as though he genuinely meant it, caught, as he was, on the hop by Bridie's appearance at his front door.

– You did ask me to pay you a visit, Bridie said.

– So I did. So I did, Ignatious admitted, inwardly scolding himself for such injudiciousness. And very delighted I am that you have decided to do so, he added, making the best of the inevitable. Do come in, he invited, standing to one side and beckoning Bridie indoors with a generous sweep of one arm. You'll have to forgive the mess. My home, you see, reflects my life: chaotic. And not even organised chaos, I fear. But then what would be the point in trying to organise the unorganisable?

Bridie stared about the small, low-ceilinged front room, mesmerised by the clutter that confronted her. Such a contrast to Mummy's neat, clinical, antiseptic way of keeping house would be hard to imagine. And Bridie loved it. She had never seen so many books. Books everywhere: piled on shelves that sagged, on chairs, on tables, on the floor. There were books on the window-sill where they jostled for occupancy with terracotta pots filled with geranium and fuchsia cuttings. Books overflowed the huge antique washing-copper that most people now used for logs. Indeed, the only place devoid of assorted tomes was the mantelpiece, and this was laden with bric-a-brac, mostly Oriental and African wood-carvings in ebony: masks, distorted animals, human shapes misshapen by the artists' symbolism. Above these hung a framed and gruesome painting depicting a pale-white succcubus reclining on an apple-green background, her breasts, knees and abdomen all imaging her woeful face, one arm thrown behind her head, her hair thick and trailing like a hirsute vine. Encircling this were smaller pictures, prints mostly, all framed in black, one of a cat dressed in scarlet robes holding a mirror in one paw, a dead white mouse in the other, its title, embossed in gold script, CHANGEABILITY. The others were equally sinister, all of people, their names, too, scripted beneath their glowering features: Mother Damnable, Louise Huebner, Anton Szandor LaVey, Sybil Leek. Bridie felt herself going cold as she looked at them, and shuddered. Yet it was as though she recognised them, had, at some clandestine, incalculable time, spoken to them. She was on the point of taking a closer look when Mr Wyett distracted her, saying: May I offer you a glass of apple juice? Home-made. Or brewed. Does one brew apple juice, do you think? he asked, clearly not expecting any reply.

– Thank you.

Mr Wyett rummaged in the corner cupboard, clanking bottles about with gusto as though indulging in a private and eccentric game of hity-tity before producing with a flourish the bottle he wanted. Here we are! he exclaimed, holding it aloft. 1980. An excellent year, he informed her with a grin, setting about filling two tumblers. People don't believe that natural juices mature with age, but they do. There's a trick to it, of course. A secret ingredient. A bit like life, wouldn't you say? Find the secret ingredient and you'll survive unscathed despite the determination of wicked forces to hasten your deterioration.

Bridie smiled, not understanding much of what he had said, but nodding anyway in agreement, taking the tumbler now offered and sniffing the golden-coloured liquid.

– How interesting, Mr Wyett observed, watching her.

Bridie looked puzzled.

– That's exactly what animals do, you know. Sniff things before they consume them.

Bridie blushed.

– Yes – oh, I beg your pardon. Do sit down, Mr Wyett invited hastily as though veering away from thoughts that troubled him, pushing a stack of books from a chair, and shoving them to one side with his foot. I must get rid of some of these, he said, mostly to himself. A purge. That is what is needed. A purge.

Bridie settled herself comfortably on the chair, and sipped her apple juice. She felt quite at home. She sensed an orderliness in the clutter. Everything welcomed her rather than tried to keep her at bay. It's really lovely, she said aloud.

– Thank you. Not bad at all, is it? Mr Wyett replied, presuming she was speaking about the drink.

– Delicious, Bridie told him, relieved, but not looking at him, eyeing instead the one book that seemed in the process of being read, lying isolated on the arm of Mr Wyett's chair, open but face down, an old, browning postcard of a beach scene, perhaps a marker, beside it. HEAR US, OH LORD, FROM HEAVEN THY DWELLING PLACE, Bridie deciphered, and wondered what on earth that could be about.

– . . . into the woods, Mr Wyett was saying.

– Pardon?

– I saw you the other day – peering into the woods, her host repeated, one eyebrow raised quizzically. You looked like Alice peering into her rabbit hole. The same expectancy on your face. The same sense of impending adventure.

– I go there quite often, Bridie told him. Almost every day. It's so lovely down there, you know. All quiet and friendly.

– Friendly? Mr Wyett obviously found that surprising.

– Yes. Very friendly.

– You must be blessed, Ignatious said almost as an aside. Have you ventured into them yet? he asked.

– Not yet, Bridie admitted, shaking her head. Although I expect I will soon.

– You expect you will soon? That sounds rather as though you are waiting for an invitation.

– I am in a way.

– And from whom do you expect it?

Bridie looked momentarily embarrassed. I'm not sure, she said. I get the feeling that there's someone waiting to meet me. Meet *me*, she stressed.

Mr Wyett's reaction to this was extraordinary. He jumped to his feet and began pacing about the room. What makes you say that, child? he demanded, coming to a halt and peering into Bridie's upturned, astonished face.

– I've no idea, Mr Wyett, she confessed warily. Just a silly feeling I have. Don't you ever get feelings about things you can't explain?

Mr Wyett nodded mournfully, and returned slowly to his chair. He sat down heavily, still nodding. Indeed I do, he told her, sounding as if he wished he didn't.

– Well, then, you know what I mean.

– Alas, only too well. Young lady – you will be most careful, won't you? he pleaded, the very quietness of his voice making his plea dramatically intense.

Bridie was surprised. Careful?

– Yes. Careful. Most careful. If ever you feel yourself being called into the woods you will take extreme care, promise me?

Bridie giggled. Why?

Mr Wyett did not immediately reply. He put his glass on the floor and leaned back in his chair, closing his eyes. The forefinger of one hand jumped erratically and he tried to control or conceal this by covering it with his other hand, making both seem joined in prayer.

– Why do you say I should take such care, Mr Wyett? Bridie insisted.

– 'There are more things in heaven and earth –', Ignatious Wyett quoted gloomily under his breath, before sitting forward again and leaning towards Bridie, trying to smile but producing more of a grimace. You might get lost, he told her tamely.

– That's not what you meant at all, Bridie told him mockingly, enforcing her disbelief by wagging a finger at him, scolding. You were going to say something quite different, weren't you?

– No, Mr Wyett told her seriously after a lengthy pause. But perhaps I meant it differently.

Without warning he burst out laughing although there was a bitter edge to his merriment. It dawned on him, perhaps for the first time, that he usually did mean things in a different way and that this, in no small measure, had been his downfall. It was the innocent refutation of his statement which made him realise that throughout his wasted, futile life his plangent, excusatory cry had been: But that's not what I meant at all! It wasn't simply a question of being misunderstood: it was rather more rarefied than that. Ignatious Wyett, through no controllable fault of his own, was prone to a sort of cerebral boiling, his thoughts seldom less than itinerant and tending to settle haphazardly upon the ears of astounded listeners who misinterpreted them if only because they were so out of place, outrageous. Since adolescence he had been accepted as an eccentric, as harmless, as even amusing. He was elevated to the ranks of 'characters' who were fast and regretfully vanishing, admittedly to the alarm of his father, a respected surgeon, and his mother, an overly zealous church-goer who had, since his birth, ordained him a priest. The problem was that Ignatious would become infatuated with the feasibility of even his most absurd ideas. He made them logical. He embellished them. They took him over.

– Now for God's sake, his dejected counsel, Daniel Kelly, told him, when you get into the witness box just answer yes or no. I want none of your daft expoundings. You're in enough trouble as it is and if you start ranting at old Corboy you can forget about leniency.

Wise words under the circumstances, but totally wasted. True, Ignatious Wyett did his best to heed the advice, even managing to sustain uncharacteristically curt, monosyllabic responses for a while. But it was a temporary respite: a casual, inoffensive observation by the prosecution triggered a hugely spectacular tirade that brought giggles and approbation from the gallery and the flushed look of apoplexy to Judge Corboy's incredulous face. For fully ten minutes he raved, partly a defence for his actions, partly an evangelical sermon of the hell-fire and brimstone variety, all the while ignoring the silent pleas from his counsel (who finally surrendered and buried his face in his arms, his body shaking, perhaps crying, perhaps laughing) and the sustained gavelling from the bench. At last, breathless, smiling broadly, he reseated himself, acknowledging the bawdy applause from the gallery with elegant waves of one hand. It didn't help his case. He was found guilty, and Judge Corboy, ordering him, with obvious relish, to be detained in prison for four years, described him scathingly as a thief and a rogue and a confidence trickster who had most wickedly abused the fear people quite rightly had for the devil to extract money from their persons.

– How could he say such things? Ignatious demanded of Daniel Kelly after the trial, hurt more, it seemed, by this slur than by his imminent incarceration.

– I told you to keep your mouth shut.

– Yes. Yes, you did. And you were quite right, Daniel, of course. But how could he call me a thief and a rogue and a confidence trickster?

– Because that's what you said you were.

– I said that? Ignatious asked, appalled.

Daniel Kelly nodded dismally. While you were ranting.

– Never! I –

– You don't listen to yourself when you talk. You admitted that you – dear God – had girded yourself to fight the devil. You admitted that you took money from several people to finance this – you know what you called it? Your labyrinthine crusade! That went down a bomb, I can tell you. And worst of all you admitted keeping the money when your lunatic crusade was a failure.

– Failure? It was not a failure.

– You said it was.

– But I didn't mean that at all. I meant it wasn't successful *yet*. Evil is ongoing. Don't you see, Daniel, wickedness is –

– Ignatious: just shut up.

– What way did you mean it? Bridie wanted to know. Mr Wyett shook his head. Then he sighed. I only wish I knew, he said, sounding very tired.

'You were going to try and remember what sort of things Mr Wyett spoke to you about,' the doctor reminds Bridie, wearing his white coat again, and sounding pleased with himself that he had not been sidetracked overnight. 'Have you remembered anything?'

Bridie is in good humour and decides to be generous.

'A little.'

'Excellent,' the doctor beams, his cheerful smiles waning in the ensuing silence. 'Are you going to tell me about it?'

'If you want me to.'

'I do indeed,' the doctor says, apparently no longer caring if it is what *she* wants, and waits, passing the time by doodling on his little pad: matchstick men in wooden attitudes.

'Well, he told me all about the woods,' Bridie reveals once she has decided she is not rushing into things. 'He really does know an awful lot about them,' she adds. 'He makes everything sound so alive. I mean, I know the trees and things are living, but Mr Wyett makes them *alive*,' she concludes, and falls silent, abandoning the doctor to make what he will of her words, and vanishing into her own hidden world, alone and content.

Mummy looked happier than she had for a very long time. You really are enjoying yourself here, aren't you, Bridie, she asked.

– Oh yes.

Mummy was pleased about that, you could see. She was a different person. I'm a different person, she told her solicitor on the phone when he called to finalise the sale of her house in the city. I feel twenty years younger, she said.

And she looked almost that much younger. Freed of city restrictions and prim attitudes, she had taken to wearing slacks and sloppy pullovers, and she let her hair hang loose. She sang little tunes to herself as she trotted about the mill, and went in for huge bunches of dried, wild flowers in a big way. She had ceased to use make-up and the harshness of features which that imposed fell away leaving her pretty rather than beautiful, leaving her looking appealingly like someone about to be beautiful. That was during the day. At night it was rather different. Alone in the huge bed she had shared with Francis she found that the pain inevitably returned, often spending the whole night tossing in anger at the loneliness that had been imposed on her, a loneliness without even a widow's grief to salve it. Cruelly, the restrictions to which she had so gaily bid good riddance left a void that became filled with yearning. At times it was as though Francis had never existed, as though she was clean and unbroken, as though she was innocent and waiting for the first embraces of ecstatic love. The stark realisation, when it came, that this was not true, made her, frequently, cry herself to sleep.

Just as she had predicted, the woods beckoned to Bridie, their mysterious rustlings and sighs as seductive and potent as the famed call of the sea that lured men towards unshaped, tacit destinies, and Bridie responded eagerly, feeling an unwonted joy at the whispered invitation. Very early in the morning, about eight weeks since their arrival in the village, she set out. A wonderful sense of adventure stung her mind: all the epic journeys she had read or heard about loomed into her consciousness – the desert, the tundra, the steaming rain-forests, great wastes of uninhabited earth all flickered and fused and dissembled in her brain, and she began to think of the woods as a vast, charmed, uncharted territory that was hers to explore. Yet, without the slightest inkling where the understanding came from, she appreciated that she must respect the authority of the trees, aware that it was she who intruded, and that their tolerance would depend on her behaviour.

Content to delay her adventure, she decided to walk the long way round, through the village instead of across the fields, telling herself it was important to identify the proximity of the houses and the shop and the small garage in order to heighten the distance of her destination.

Despite the early hour there was considerable activity. Miss Calilly, midget-sized and ugly as an arrowfish, bounced over the cobbles on her bicycle, pring-pringing her bell through the street as though she was the village's mobile, early-morning alarm, her bewildered Jack Russell propped in the basket on the handlebars, her odd, protruding eyes, flicking only briefly, suspiciously over Bridie, fixed on some distant objective. Further on, past a group of five cottages built in a half-moon, between the garage that displayed a broken tractor, a dilapidated hearse and Brian Smith's Zephyr on its forecourt, and the shop where Mrs Canty fussily shooed an argumentative tabby cat from the window, a plot of land had been neatly pegged out, each peg linked to the next by lengths of orange, plastic-coated, bailing-string. There, Toby Dixon already toiled, pedgilling relentlessly with pick and shovel in his efforts to excavate an atomic shelter although, pushing eighty, his prospects of completing his masterpiece were slim. Opposite was another cluster of cottages, terraced labourers' homes now converted, then a spinney of willows, a small pond on which a dabchick floated and finally, in grand isolation, as though purposely withdrawing from village life, Mr Wyett's cottage with curtains still drawn. Bridie tutted to herself, mentally scolding Mr Wyett for staying in bed so late.

Just outside the village proper but within its geographic boundary, hidden by a bend in the road, a circle of well-tended grass surrounded a small stone monument commemorating the wasteful demise of young men from the village in some forgotten, savage war: at the base, a withered wreath of holly, berryless, the leaves brown and dry, brittle as unoiled leather. Near it, two women stood talking. The younger of the two, a strapping girl, huge-breasted and sulky, carried a basket of kindling-wood on her shoulder as easily and gracefully as some nomadic bedouin. She eyed Bridie with suspicion.

– Good morning, Bridie said politely.

Both women bowed their heads a little by way of acknowledging and returning the greeting, but neither of them spoke as though so to do might involve them in some inextricable complication. When Bridie had passed, they whispered to each other and held hands, and Bridie was glad she had left them behind.

Then (telling herself she had been miraculously transported there) she had reached the boundary of the woods. Quietly, almost on tiptoe, she entered, humming gently an improvised tune to alert the trees to her unannounced arrival. Within yards of the track the silence was total, and each step that Bridie took shattered the stillness as small, dry twigs snapped under her weight. Tiny insects, some furry as pussy willow, all still numbed by the chill residue of the night, flew dazedly past her, then turned back and hovered before her face, peering at her for a moment, dancing in agitation, before fluttering away again only to be immediately replaced by others, curious and belligerent. It was as if every drowsy, shimmering insect in the region had been sent to goggle and report on this outrageous intruder. Then, as rapidly as they had appeared, they were gone, evaporating it seemed, along with the fine, web-strewn mist, as the sun gradually gained height and warmth, leaving the air clear and unblemished and wonderfully scented.

. . . The air in the house got more and more fetid and musty as Mummy refused to open the windows. Upstairs, the child, four years younger than Bridie, wrapped in a plain white nightdress that had already taken on the lachrymose semblance of a shroud, coughed and coughed and grew steadily weaker, her body shrinking and seeming to be consumed by the deep, soft mattress, the blankets stretched tight and level across the bed and showing no hint of an occupant.

Mummy got very peculiar and Bridie worried about her; she worried about Daddy too who was forever getting the sharp edge of Mummy's tongue, and spent more and more time away from the home.

Soon the house stank of medicines and potions, and of the choking, cloying, heavy-scented lavender water that Mummy sprinkled about the place, making a pathetic little ceremony of it, tapping the neck of the bottle with her forefinger, her head bowed, her shoulders hunched, her bearing that of some mournful alchemist trying, possibly, to persuade the sweet, heavy scent to remind her of country gardens, and youth, and happier times. Each morning she saw Bridie off to school, shutting the door quickly behind her in case something evil slipped in; and every afternoon she was there waiting to let Bridie in again, immediately bolting the door. She spent nearly all her waking hours upstairs with 'poor Charlotte', reading to her from a slim book that she carried everywhere with her as though her daugher's survival was somehow linked to the monotonous turning of the pages, or just talking to her, telling her monstrously exaggerated tales of what was happening downstairs and using these fabrications to put her longings into words, making her feel wanted and 'still an integral part of the family' as she put it, or merely sitting still and silent in the straight-backed, cane-and-wickerwork chair beside the bed, staring at the irrevocable, plodding approach of death, often with a furious anger in her eyes, sometimes with tears streaming down her cheeks. Three times each day she fed Charlotte, spooning the pappy substance of mashed vegetables and minced meat into her mouth, scraping the dribbled matter upwards from her chin and forcing it between her teeth, then wiping the thin, blue, unreceptive lips and washing the rest of her face diligently with a damp flannel (Bridie! Dampen the flannel for Mummy with warm water, will you? *Warm* water, mind. Not hot) when each meal was done, accepting the unintelligible grunts as a sign of gratitude and love.

– How's Charlotte today? Bridie asked every single day, dutifully.

– Still the same, Bridie.

– Has the doctor been?

– Yes. But she's past the help of doctors now.

– She's going to die, isn't she?

– Only if we let her, Bridie, Mummy said in a strange, far-away voice as if she had the power to control such things.

– Only if we let her?

– Yes, darling.

But Charlotte died anyway, wizened and pinched and shrivelled like an ancient crone. She looked frightened in death, and the fear appalled Bridie who had been led to believe there would be nothing but calm and serenity.

Bridie was pleased when they finally got around to burying Charlotte. Once she had been allowed to see her dead sister in her pretty white shroud, cushioned comfortably for the journey on padded white silk and with a posy in her stiff little hands (still wearing the silver and pearl ring that Mummy had given her and which Bridie always envied), and had watched the lid being lowered and screwed down, she dismissed all memory of her sister from her mind, banishing even the recall of the happy moments they had spent together. Within a week it was as though Charlotte had never existed . . .

Mummy went quite funny for a while, taking to locking herself away in her bedroom and thumping the pillows for hours on end; and Daddy started drinking far too much, often not going to bed but dozing fitfully in his armchair. For ages they didn't speak to each other although Daddy did try. But he was always cut off short with a withering, hateful look.

Bridie beathed deeply, holding the fresh, woodland air in her lungs for as long as was bearable, her cheeks puffed out. Then, slowly, she opened her mouth and let the air escape, watching it steam away from her, her breath and the breathing of the woods becoming one. By now the sun had succeeded in seeping through the trees, shafts of its light making the cobwebs, slung like fairy hammocks between the lower branches and across the bright-green, new tendrils of the wild blackberry-bushes, stand out, delicate and crystal clear. As it gathered strength (caught fire, Bridie thought for some obscure reason), it lent a new and lustrous colour to the leaves that tumbled from time to time, unable to bear the weight of the overnight moisture. Bridie reached out and caught one as it fell close to her. She examined it carefully, feeling the chamois-like texture of its flesh, fascinated by the tiny veins so intricately patterned; she held it aloft and gazed at this new miracle with the sun behind it. Then she opened her fingers and let it continue its journey to the ground, watching it loop-the-loop downwards and settle. She was still watching it when it began to move.

At first she supposed it was nothing more than some gentle breeze which she could not feel that shifted the leaf; yet none of the other leaves scattered about were moving. It was almost as if the tiny leaf were having spasms, lurching a little way, jerkily, and then stopping, exhausted. She crouched down on her hunkers, her elbows on her knees, cupping her chin in her hands, and grinned hugely in delight as she spotted the ants, outriders of some nearby colony, sent to ship the vegetation on a voyage only they could navigate.

– It's like a journey, darling, Granny insisted on explaining the night of Charlotte's funeral, determined to impart her knowledge of the hereafter.

– A journey? Bridie asked, not all that interested, but willing to gratify Granny who she quite liked and who seemed to be enjoying herself.

– Yes, Bridie, Granny confirmed, pursing her lips and nodding to emphasise how positive she was. Jesus sends His holy angels to gather up little souls and carry them home to a peaceful land, to that place we have visited before in our dreams and where we felt contented and secure.

– I've never visited anywhere in my dreams, Bridie pointed out, suddenly alarmed that without her own place she might have to face the prospect of spending eternity drifting endlessly.

– You will, Granny assured her, patting her on the head. You will. Everyone does. Wonderful travels they are too, she added wistfully and gazing away as though browsing through some particularly appealing astral brochure. I promise you that you'll have those dreams before Jesus wants you to die.

– But supposing I don't – where would I go? Bridie persisted, still seeing herself meandering in space like a gypsy.

– Don't fret so, child. You'll find your place. Everyone does. Eventually.

– Mother, I wish you wouldn't fill Bridie's head with that nonsense, Mummy said, coming into the room suddenly.

– It's not nonsense, dear, Granny said.

– It is for me.

– A lot of things are – for you, Granny said tightly and looked satisfied when Mummy blushed and started fiddling with her hair. You just listen to your Granny, Bridie, and you'll see.

– Yes, Granny, Bridie said.

– Good girl.

As Bridie moved deeper into the woods the birds began to chatter again, rested after the doze they had taken since their early-morning chorus. An aggressive, golden-beaked blackbird was shrillest, plummeting between the trees and using their great, lichen-covered trunks to ricochet his persistent, piercing warning of a stranger, fluffing his feathers and throwing out his chest in a show of belligerence. Smaller birds, braver it seemed, or just more curious, flew closer, skipping from branch to branch, cocking their heads and regarding her with bright, beady, impertinent eyes, almost daring her to put their bravery to the test. High above, a flock of rooks, warned by the crackled code of their private sentry, left the cover of a great beech and circled in the sky, calling raucously, then wheeled and settled down once more, pacified or confident of their ability to deal with this unexpected intruder. Then, suddenly, total silence fell again. Nothing moved. Everything froze in attitudes of motionless attention. Squinting, Bridie saw the owl eyeing her with suspicion.

– You're very quiet, Mummy pointed out. What have you been up to all day?

– Walking.

Mummy gave one of her high, tinkling, forced little laughs: the ones she gave when puzzled while pretending not to be. Just walking? That's what you tell me every day.

– That's what I do every day.

– And where did you walk to?

– The woods.

– Again?

– I went *into* them today, Bridie pointed out.

– That's nice, darling.

– And I saw an owl.

– How lovely! Mummy exclaimed, but then most things to Mummy were lovely if they didn't inconvenience her.

– And I spoke to it.

– How sweet, Mummy said, setting her electric whisker in motion and assiduously studying a recipe-book.

– It's not really an owl, you know.
– What was that, dear?
– It's not really an owl, Bridie repeated, raising her voice above the din.
– Isn't it? – Damn! Mummy snapped as some of the mixture spurted from the bowl on to her blouse.
– It's really a lovely lady in disguise.
Mummy switched off the machine and set about removing the splotches of cake-mix from her blouse with her fingertips. A lady in disguise? Oh, dear.
Bridie nodded seriously. That's right.
– And how do you make that out? Mummy wanted to know, dabbing the stains with a damp cloth.
– She told me.
Mummy thought that was really very amusing, and started to laugh gaily. Really Bridie! You *do* have a great imagination. Told you, indeed.
– It's true. That's what it said just before it vanished.
– Oh, it vanished?
– Yes. One minute it was there on the branch and the next minute it was gone.
That seemed to bring something to Mummy's mind. She stopped dabbing for a moment and stood quite still, just gazing out of the window. Then she shrugged, and threw the cloth into the sink. A trick of the light, darling. That's all it was, she decided. A trick of the light.
– I don't think so.
– I'm sure it was.

Ignatious Wyett, on the other hand, reacted rather differently. He accepted Bridie's story albeit cautiously, and when she had finished he sighed deeply as though resigning himself to consequences he had already reluctantly foreseen.
And it was this intrepid application of resigning himself to the uncontrollable future that made his years in prison bearable. Indeed, when he thought about it later, he quite enjoyed them, manipulating any hardship to his advantage,

often, in a sense, glossing over it by pretending to be someone else – Oscar Wilde, Raoul Wallenberg, Nelson Mandela – and lumbering them with whatever pain his incarceration inflicted on his spirit, often standing below the high, barred window, gazing at the glimpse of sky, his arms folded behind his back, quoting aloud what he could remember of Wilde's *De Profundis*, or sermonising as Wallenberg might have done only to some invisible angelic congregation, or propounding quasi-political stratagem that would eradicate the profound stupidity of apartheid. Curiously, his own ludicrous actions which had landed him there never warranted his consideration: he banished them totally from his mind, sustaining himself on the wrongful conviction of his unaware figurants. And there was never any question of his being ill-treated, far from it: so bizarre was his crime that the warders (decent enough men clearly chosen more for their physical strength than for any intellectual acumen) regarded him askance and left him pretty much to his own devices lest, perhaps, he *had* some intimacy with the supernatural, and might use this to revenge himself of any supposed cruelty, while his fellow inmates (a cheery, devil-may-care lot, forgers, cat-burglars, unlicensed pedlars and the like) immediately installed him as a sort of gullible guru vaguely hopeful that his past dealings with the occult had given him some oblique power which they could persuade him to use to their benefit.

All in all, Ignatious Wyett had a pretty easy time and far from being released scarred and bitter, he had emerged (one year early for good behaviour, having bowled the probation committee over with a carefully rehearsed dissertation on his profound repentance) refreshed and with a spring in his step as though he had simply undergone some self-imposed, if mildly severe retreat.

Emboldened, then, and quite pleased with himself for having survived his ordeal unscathed, he sallied forth, as he immediately thought of it, while the great, metal gates clanged shut behind him, to face the world and put his life together again. He soon learned, however, that his punishment actually started on his release. His erstwhile friends shunned him lest contact with such a reprobate would taint their good name also. His parents, still mortally embarrassed, wanted nothing to do with him, preferring to settle their parental love in cash. Indeed, it wasn't long before he found himself suffering an isolation far greater than any he had endured in prison. Yet, although hurt, he was in no way angry, accepting his ostracisation stoically, telling himself it was but another of life's capricious burdens. Without fuss, malice or regret he disposed of what belongings he found redundant, accepted his father's generous bribe, and folded his tent, creeping unobtrusively from the city without a single farewell, and settled in the village where nobody knew him.

'What else did this Mr Wyett tell you about?' the doctor would like to know, please.

Bridie shrugs. 'Things.'

The doctor taps the pen on his thumb-nail and smiles tolerantly, confident that Bridie will get round to telling him all he wants to know in her own circuitous time. And he smiles knowingly to himself when she starts to speak again.

'You know why Mr Wyett was special?' she asks. 'Because when I told him what the owl said to me – about really being a lady, I mean, he didn't laugh or anything. He listened to me and understood.'

'I didn't laugh at you either, Bridie.'

'No. But you think there's something wrong with me.'

'Is there?'

'*I* don't think so.'

'You find nothing strange in what you did?'

'No.'

The doctor gazes at her for several seconds in silence before returning to his original theme. 'We were talking about you and Mr Wyett.'

Bridie frowns as though she has forgotten that. Then she brightens. 'Oh. Yes.'

'Was there anything else that made him special?'

'He liked me.'

The doctor blinks. 'A lot of people must have liked you.'

'No.' Bridie said but not as if perturbed. 'Well, not the way Mr Wyett liked me.'

'What made his – his liking different?'

'The things he said.'

The doctor waits.

'Do you know what he told me?'

The doctor still waits.

'He told me – much later when he knew me better – he told me that . . .' Bridie stops abruptly and stares at the doctor.

'Told you?' the doctor encourages, pen now poised to record the information for future, clinical evaluation.

But Bridie has once again gone away, her eyes blank and lifeless, her hands folded and motionless on her lap.

Not that Bridie told Mr Wyett quite the same story as she told her mother. That would have been silly. One had to change things for people, making allowances for their ability to understand. Mummy didn't seem to mind if what she heard was the truth or not, so long as she liked and understood what was said. Mr Wyett was different. He only wanted the truth, and Bridie gave it to him as best she could.

· TWO ·

THE FINAL FEW weeks of winter were particularly harsh. Although the snow that had been forecast never arrived, the frost was wickedly severe, freezing even, it seemed, what little sap remained in the bodies of the trees, making their branches brittle, ready to be snapped off and hurled willy-nilly to the ground by the bitter east wind that swept relentlessly up the narrow valley. The smaller wild animals suffered dreadfully, more and more forced to seek nourishment close to the village, scudding about the farmyards like dry, brown leaves in the baleful moonlight, ransacking the grain-barns and feasting nervously in the bags of layer's mash. The great owl, too, left its cover on nightly raids, gliding silently across the sky before diving on some unsuspecting, injudicious rodent. As ever, its appearances made the old people shudder and take prodigious care of themselves, grittily determined to deny it their lives. But since legend dictated that someone must die, it was with a sorrow tinged with thankfulness that they received the news that little Oliver Lynch had been found dead in his cot; and their grief, although genuine, had a fractious intensity about it as though the sorrow they had been hoarding for their own kith could now safely be donated to the dead child with impunity. They attended the funeral and brought flowers; they linked arms and wept openly; yet all the while there was a glint of triumph in their eyes.

It was warm and cosy and friendly in Mr Wyett's front room. Logs crackled and spat on the fire, and the books glowed in the blue and green and yellow light and seemed to give off a heat of their own. Bridie looked very small in the huge, over-stuffed, winged armchair, but she was very contented and waited for Mr Wyett to continue their conversation. He had made tea for a change which Bridie liked, feeling very grown-up as she balanced the saucer on her knee, sipping delicately from the thin, porcelain cup. Mr Wyett rather slurped his, but she didn't mind since he seemed to be enjoying it that way: he seemed to be playing for time, too, which was curious, taking ages to drain his cup. Finally he did, however.

– Can you describe it to me, child? he asked quietly, his voice distant as though he suspected the answer might be one he would rather not hear.

– Well, Bridie began, and frowned in concentration, liking to get things right for Mr Wyett. I looked up through the sun and saw the owl. It was huge, Mr Wyett. A huge big owl, brown and silver – its wings were silver. It was sitting in a big tree with its head all twisted to one side. Not actually looking at me, but *seeming* to look at me.

Mr Wyett nodded his understanding.

– Then I suppose I must have looked away, or blinked maybe, because the next thing I saw was that the owl had gone and there was this lovely lady standing under the same tree. She was all shiny and silver – dressed all in silvery clothes, I mean.

– Did she look like anyone you know, Bridie? Or like anyone you used to know? Mr Wyett asked.

Bridie looked confused. I don't know, she confessed. You see, she didn't seem to have a face.

Mr Wyett looked startled.

– As far as I can remember it was covered with something. A hood, I think.

Mr Wyett relaxed, feeling better.

– Like a magic cloak with a hood that made her not there, Bridie went on. Or not *necessarily* there, she added.

Mr Wyett didn't seem to understand that.

Bridie tried again. It was like she could make herself be seen only by people she wanted to see her. She just wasn't there at all for anyone else.

– But she didn't speak to you?

Bridie shook her head. No, she said firmly.

Mr Wyett appeared to have a load taken off his mind.

– Well, I don't think so, Bridie put in.

Mr Wyett gave a small, involuntary groan. The nerve in his finger started to jerk and he clamped his hand into a fist, thumping the arm of his chair but not violently. The old postcard that Bridie had presumed to be a bookmark, still there after all this time, fell to the floor. Mr Wyett retrieved it and tore it up, tossing the pieces into the fire. He waited until it had burned completely before asking: What do you mean by that, Bridie?

– Oh, dear, Bridie said, looking from the ashes to Mr Wyett's face, trying to find some reason for his action in his eyes but finding nothing except curiosity, that's very hard to explain. I don't remember actually *hearing* any words. I don't think she *said* anything the way we say things, but . . . I don't know, Mr Wyett. I didn't hear anything but I seemed to *understand* what she wanted me to understand. Like she was whispering inside my head.

– And what was it you understood?

Bridie smiled shyly. That she wanted to be my friend, she answered quietly. And that she wanted me to be hers, she added, lowering her head, wondering if she was sounding boastful, hoping she wasn't.

Indeed, Bridie's feeling seemed to be the furthest thing from Mr Wyett's mind. He looked stunned. His eyes became glazed and the blood seemed to drain from his face leaving it ashen. He moaned quietly to himself, then went very quiet and still, not even, it appeared, breathing. And the room, too, Bridie felt, held its breath, the great exposed timbers stiffening, the eyes on the ugsome faces in the prints alight.

Bridie was mesmerised. She was also bewildered that what to her had been something magical and delightful should bring about such an eerie reaction. She felt saddened and worried about Mr Wyett who now looked so terribly woebegone, like he had suddenly come face to face with catastrophe, like Daddy had looked a couple of times.

– I know. Don't tell me. You've been out walking again, Mummy said happily as she spooned the soft pap into the baby's gaping mouth.

– That's right, Bridie admitted.

– And it was in the woods.

Bridie nodded. Yes.

Mummy looked pleased with her perspicacity. Did you see your owl?

– No, Bridie lied.

– Oh dear. What a shame. Well, never mind. It was probably sleeping. Owls are supposed to sleep during the day, you know. They're called nocturnal.

– Yes. I know.

Mummy looked a bit hurt that her knowledge was nothing new. Pass me that napkin, will you?

Bridie passed the napkin, and Mummy started to wipe the baby's chin. Who's a great little man? she wanted to know, and Oliver gurgled contentedly at the compliment. Then Mummy set her toes firmly on the floor and bounced him on her knee: Ride a cock horse to Banbury Cross . . .

– Ride a cock horse to Banbury Cross, Daddy said in his silly singsong voice and Bridie chuckled. To see a fine lady upon a white horse, Daddy went on, his strong hands holding her steady on his bouncing knees, his thumbs pressing gently and moving a little on her tiny breasts. Rings on her fingers and bells on her toes: Daddy supported her with one hand as the other tickled her toes. She shall have music wherever she goes: Daddy's fingers had scuttled to her knee and were creeping playfully upwards towards her thigh, his eyes bright, his smile fixed.

He was still bestowing that frozen smile on Bridie when Mummy came into the room, noiselessly in her fluffy felt slippers, and snatched Bridie away despite her protests. It's high time you were in bed, young lady, she said to Bridie without looking at her, reserving her angry glare for poor Daddy who had suddenly wilted and looked very upset and fumbled in his pockets. Bridie heard him blowing his nose as Mummy carried her upstairs, and there was something fierce and determined about the way she tucked the blankets in under the mattress.

– I want Daddy to tuck me in, Bridie said.

– Not tonight, Mummy snapped.

– Why not?

– That's why, Mummy told her.

Bridie decided to scream.

– Now you just stop that, Bridie Lynch, Mummy shouted, calling her Bridie Lynch like she always did when very angry. I want none of your stupid nonsense.

– I want Daddy.

– Well you can't have him.

'You were telling me all the things Mr Wyett told you about,' the doctor is saying, not keen to let Bridie off the hook.

'I've told you,' Bridie says, annoyed that he is still harping on the same subject.

'Not everything, I don't think.'

'What else do you want to know?'

'Whatever you want to tell me. You were about to say something more –'

'Oh yes.'

The doctor waits.

So does Bridie.

'Will you tell me?' The doctor breaks first.

'Yes.'

'Thank you.'

Bridie makes him wait just a little longer, passing the time by playing a silent melody on her knees with her fingers, like on a piano.

– You've no ear whatever, Bridie Lynch, the music teacher said in a loud voice.

– Bridie Lynch has no ears, the girls teased her, clapping their hands over their ears and making monstrous faces.

– That's why she couldn't hear her father sneaking off in the middle of the night, Patricia Brazier had to put in – her being the smart one.

– He didn't sneak off in the night, Bridie yelled, her eyes brimming with furious tears. He's away on business. In Egypt.

That shut them up: Egypt was a place no one could argue with.

'Well,' Bridie says finally, using that firm, clipped voice she has noticed adults using when they know what they are talking about. 'He liked to talk to me about spirity things.'

The doctor's body gives a little jerk. 'Spirity things?' he asks.

'That's right. You know.'

The doctor issues a small, perplexed laugh. 'I'm afraid I don't, Bridie.'

Bridie bows her head graciously as if she appeciates his difficulty. 'Well,' she says again, 'you know that everything has a spirit, don't you?'

The doctor allows that he does, hesitantly.

'Not just people,' Bridie reminds him. 'The trees and animals – they have spirits too, just like ours.'

The doctor accepts that, nodding.

'And, like with people, there are good spirits and bad spirits.'

The doctor sees the logic in that and continues to nod.

'That's what Mr Wyett told me about.'

'About good and bad spirits?'

'That's right.'

The doctor crumples his brow, appearing to think. He strokes either side of his nose with thumb and forefinger, an action that seems to irritate Bridie: to stop it, she offers further clarification. 'He didn't want me to make a mistake and become too friendly with the wrong sort of spirit.'

'Oh,' the doctor remarks, releasing his nose and writing that down. 'I see.'

Bridie gives him a tolerant smile. 'You don't *really*,' she says in a good-natured way.

The doctor returns her smile. 'No, I don't *really*,' he admits, raising his eyebrows in hope of an explanation.

'I'm not surprised. It took me quite a long time.'

'But you understand now what he meant?'

'Oh yes.'

'Will you help me to understand?'

'I might.'

The doctor waits again patiently.

After several minutes' silence, Bridie gives him a quick look and straightens up in her chair as though it has just dawned on her that he is waiting. 'Oh, not *now*, doctor,' she says. 'Not this minute.'

The doctor looks crestfallen. 'Oh. Why not now, Bridie?'

'I'll have to talk it over.'

'With?'

'Lady, of course. Who else?'

Bridie stared in amazement at the apparition. Oddly, she was in no way frightened, accepting the sudden materialisation of the Silver Lady as just another element of the magic that surrounded her, another wonder of the mystical woods.

– Hello, she said politely, and the lady moved her hand in acknowledgement. That was when Bridie first sensed the lady speaking to her in her head: Hello, she seemed to reply. My, what a pretty little girl.

– Thank you, said Bridie.

– And how kind of you to come and visit us here.

– I love it here.

– Yes. Yes, it is nice, isn't it?

– It's lovely, Bridie affirmed.

The lady threw back her head and gave a tinkling laugh, silver like her shimmering clothes. I can see we are going to be great friends, she said. You will be my friend, won't you, Bridie?

– Oh yes, Bridie agreed readily. Then: You know my name!

– Of course, my dear.

– Do you know everything?

– No. Not everything.

The lady moved forward and seemed about to touch Bridie on the cheek, but at the last moment she desisted, lowering her arm again, sadly, it struck Bridie.

– Did she touch you, Bridie? Mr Wyett wanted to know as soon as he had recovered his composure.

– No, Bridie told him. I think she was going to but changed her mind at the last minute.

– Ah, sighed Mr Wyett.

– She seemed very sad.

– Ah, Mr Wyett sighed again. You are certain she never touched you?

– Quite certain. Why?

Mr Wyett shook his head. No matter, he said, dismissing the question with a wave that knocked the book from the arm of his chair. He leaned down and retrieved it, stroking it. He opened the flap of the dust-jacket and produced a dried dragon-fly wing which he inserted as a marker. Hear us Oh Lord, he said mostly to himself.

– Pardon? asked Bridie, generously giving him a chance to tell the truth.

– Just the title, Mr Wyett explained, becoming flustered again, holding up the book for Bridie to see. HEAR US, OH LORD, FROM HEAVEN THY DWELLING PLACE, he said aloud.

– Oh, said Bridie, hoping that this acceptance of his lie would put him at his ease again.

Why on earth she had chosen to locate her father in Egypt of all places, Bridie had no idea. She knew nothing about the place: it was simply a name that came to her on the spur of the moment. And yet, uncannily, there it was: proof that she had been correct; three months after Daddy had gone away (taking very little with him: two large and one small suitcase; looking very miserable but trying to be brave, kissing Bridie and shaking hands formally with Mummy who had offered her hand first saying 'We might as well try and be civilised about it', and driving off in the taxi without looking back) a postcard from Cairo with 'My love to you and Oliver and Mummy' scrawled on the back.

– There you are, Patricia Brazier, Bridie said haughtily, shoving the postcard under her best friend's nose. I told you my Daddy had gone to Egypt on business.

Which solved one problem (the girls in her class now forced to hold her in some esteem: who could tell what other wonders she might produce: a parent in Egypt, no less, and Bridie herself more than likely to visit him there in the holidays, as she pointed out, and see camels and elephants and tigers and bring back exotic jewels and fabulous clothes and wonderful perfumes which she might, if they were nice to her, share) but did nothing to ease the tension at home. If anything, it made matters worse, setting Mummy off again:

– It's so damn typical, Bridie heard her complain to Granny a few evenings after the postcard had arrived. Swanning about in Cairo and leaving me to clear up the mess here at home.

– I think Francis has been most generous to you, Kathleen, Granny said, taking the wrong side as usual. He's given you everything. The house. The furniture. The custody of the children – all without a murmur.

– Hah, Mummy scoffed. Fat chance he'd have had of getting custody. What the hell is he *doing* in Cairo? she asked, not expecting an answer.

– I'm sure he has his reasons for being there. He's got to make a new life for himself, poor man. The question I want answered is what are you going to do? You've got to get yourself straightened out, my girl.

– I'm making my plans.

– And what might they be?

– I haven't decided yet. Not fully. I'm selling this for a start, Mummy said, somehow making it clear that 'this' was the house.

– And moving where? Granny wanted to know.

– I'm not sure. Away. Out of the city, I think.

Bridie, listening, liked the sound of that.

Granny didn't seem to. You in the country? she asked. I can't see you living in the country, Kathleen.

– Why ever not?

– You'll never cope. Granny was adamant.

– Of course I'll cope.

– That's it, of course, Granny said, as if the idea had just struck her. You've never been able to cope.

Mummy sounded livid when she replied: I might have coped better if you hadn't taken Francis's side all the time.

Granny gave a hard, cackling laugh. Oh, yes. Blame me. Blame your mother. First it's Francis, now it's me. Blame everyone but yourself.

– I don't want to blame anyone, Mummy replied.

– Well, you have a queer way of showing it, my girl.

– I'm sorry, mother.

– Oh, that's all right, Granny said in her haughty voice that meant it clearly was not all right. I'll not say another word. You do whatever you think is best, but don't come crying to me if you make another mistake.

– For heaven's sake –

– I've had my say.

– Can't you ever see things from *my* side, mother? Ever?

Bridie, on the stairs, could imagine Granny blessing herself before saying: I only see the truth, Kathleen, even if it hurts.

– And what about Bridie's schooling? Granny actually said.

– What about it?

– What sort of education do you think the child will get in some silly little country school?

– She won't be going to any silly little country school.

– Oh? What, then, may I ask?

– She's going to boarding-school in September.

– Indeed? Very high and mighty, I must say.

– It will be good for her.

– Huh. And what about between now and September?

Mummy's confident tones faltered. She – with all the upset – I thought – with the move and everything – I got her a doctor's certificate to absent her until she goes to boarding school.

– So the child is to run wild until –

– She won't be running wild.

– And what *doctor* – Granny stressed the word, impregnating it with quackery – would give such a certificate.

– A friend of mine, Mummy snapped.

– I might have guessed as much.

'Let's talk about something different today, Bridie,' the doctor suggests. It is the fifth day and he sounds fatigued: looking forward to the weekend, Bridie supposes.

'All right, doctor.'

'That's another thing: why don't you call me by my name. Joseph. It's a bit friendlier.'

'I prefer doctor, doctor,' Bridie says stiffly.

Rebuffed, the doctor blushes. 'Fine. If you prefer that,' he says, immediately launching into today's subject. 'I would like you to tell me more about your family.'

Bridie inclines her head, expressing tolerant agreement.

'When your father left, did you and your mother become closer?'

Bridie thinks about that. 'No. Not really,' she answers finally. 'Mummy said she wanted us to. I mean, she said we should get to know each other better, and become friends.'

'But you didn't?'

'We couldn't.'

'Why was that?'

Bridie gives one of her shrugs. 'Mummy was busy with Oliver most of the time,' she says, but something in her tone implies that this isn't the real reason; not all of it anyway.

'Was that the only reason?' the doctor asks, spotting the implication.

'Yes,' Bridie lies.

'Did that upset you?'

'No. Of course not.'

'You didn't mind your mother giving all her attention to your baby brother?'

'She didn't give him *all* her attention. I never said that.'

The doctor consults his notes. 'Well, most of her time, then. Didn't you mind that?'

'Why should I?'

'Lots of girls your age would mind. They might feel left out. Or unloved.'

Bridie laughs. 'I didn't *need* love, doctor. Not from Mummy anyway. Daddy gave me all the love I needed.'

'But he had left you.'

'He left Mummy. Not me.'

'Oh yes. I remember you said that. So you weren't jealous of Oliver?'

'No,' Bridie snaps, getting irritated.

'Did you like Oliver?'

Bridie makes a clicking noise with her tongue and looks away. 'Everybody likes babies,' she says loftily, as if regarding the question as spurious.

(– Bridie, hold Oliver for two secs, will you, while I get his cot ready? Mummy asked.

Bridie took the baby on her knee. He smelled nice after his bath and a good dousing of baby-powder. She bounced him up and down and sang the words of 'Ride a cock horse', quietly. Oliver grinned and gurgled and dribbled. Bridie bounced him harder, her knees rising higher each time and thumping down hard again, while Oliver's head snapped back and forth wildly. He began to cry. Bridie kept on bouncing him, gripping him fiercely. Oliver screamed. Bridie started to shake him. Then she heard Mummy hurrying from the nursery and stopped the ride: she held Oliver close to her, his head over her shoulder, patting him on the back, crooning.

– Dear me, Mummy said, smiling at the loving scene, I thought you were murdering him the way he was screaming.

Bridie smiled back, her eyes wide and innocent.

– Probably wind, Mummy said.

– I don't think so. He's been burping on my shoulder.

– Aaaah, Mummy said kindly. I expect the wee chap is just tired, then.

– I expect so, Bridie agreed, passing Oliver to Mummy.

– Thank you, darling, Mummy said.)

The doctor smiles indulgently. 'Not everyone.'

Bridie ignores that.

'So you liked Oliver?'

'Yes.'

'Then why did you kill him?'

Bridie awoke completely alert as if her consciousness had been snapped on by a switch. Away in the distance, the vixen screamed her troubled quest for a mate, curdling the night with her shrill melancholy. Bridie smiled to herself and snuggled down contentedly between the warm sheets, waiting. Over the months, an understanding, an intimacy had developed between herself and the vixen: a curious arrangement unfettered by the fact that they had never seen each other. In the darkness, Bridie had delegated her loneliness to the forlorn creature and, now, it was as though it acted on her behalf when crying for companionship at the night.

Soon the eerie pleading stopped, and Bridie felt a tingle of excitement. She sat up in bed, propping her pillow comfortably behind her head, her eyes wide open and eager. It wasn't long before the expected shadow came into her room, hanging for a moment in the brightness of the moon, allowing itself to be recognised. Then it moved into the darkness of the corner, and Bridie knew it had settled there.

For a moment Bridie looks startled and puzzled as though genuinely not understanding the question. Then she relaxes and gives a little smile. 'Oh *that*. It was the only way.'

'I don't quite follow,' the doctor says.

'Lady said it had to be done. She said it was the only way.'

'And that's the reason you killed Oliver – because Lady said it had to be done?'

'Of course,' Bridie insists, sounding surprised.

'You'll have to explain that to me some more, Bridie.' The doctor keeps his voice carefully modulated to deflect any horror or shock he feels.

Bridie cocks her head. 'Explain what?' she asks.

'What you just told me. Why did your Lady say it had to be done? What reason did she give?'

'Oh,' says Bridie, taking her time and using it to push a strand of wayward hair from her face and tuck it neatly behind one of her ears. 'Oh,' she repeats.

Bridie stayed stock-still, her eyes fixed on the dark corner into which the shadow had settled, her mouth slightly open, not daring to even breathe. Nor blink: she stared and stared into the blackness, concentrating. Soon her eyes were filled with millions of tiny lights, twinkling. Then the lights merged and her Silver Lady was standing there by her bed, her arms outstretched, and Bridie felt a lovely warmness consume her body.

' "Oh" ', the doctor repeats. 'Is that all you have to say?' he asks, sounding disappointed but not displeased.

'I'm thinking,' Bridie tells him sharply.

The doctor nods an apology.

'Expedient,' Bridie says out of the blue.

'Expedient?' Doctor Joseph repeats, looking as though he is wondering where on earth that word has come from.

Bridie nods. 'That's the word she used. Expedient,' she repeats, letting the syllables roll off her tongue as though tasting them.

The doctor scribbles that down.

'Oliver's death was expedient,' Bridie enlarges.

'Did she say why?'

Bridie shakes her head. 'Not exactly. She's not really given to explanations.'

'What *did* she tell you?' Doctor Joseph persists quite sharply, as though he feels he is on to something.

'Just what I told you. That it was expedient.'

'But when I asked you if she told you *why* it was expedient you said "not exactly". So, she must have said something more.'

Bridie shifts on her chair, finally hooking her feet about its legs and leaning forward. 'Nothing more,' she asserts blatantly, looking the doctor in the eye.

'You're sure?'

'Quite sure.'

The doctor sighs. 'I don't think I can believe that, Bridie.'

Bridie unhooks her feet and leans back, allowing a tiny smile to crimp her lips. Gradually she sees the doctor's confidence waver, and decides to continue sitting there, saying nothing, staring at him.

It was very strange and very wonderful: the Silver Lady said nothing but Bridie could feel and interpret without difficulty the messages she transmitted. And there was more to it than that. It wasn't just words that pattered in her mind. Images took shape. Like rapid, brilliant performances they took to the stage, impressed her, and then dissembled, followed by another almost immediately, rotating like a magic kaleidoscope, but never confusing, each sequence irrevocably linked in theme to the one preceding it. Bridie felt herself tremble with excitement. She wanted to leap from her bed and run to the lady, to embrace her, to love her. And perhaps the lady sensed this, for suddenly she lowered her arms and took a step backwards, and her shimmering silverness seemed less bright. Then, in the twinkling of an eye, she was gone, and immediately the great winged shadow left the darkness and hovered for a moment over the spot where Lady had stood. Then it, too, was gone, out of the window and away, away and up towards the stars; away, gliding majestically on the currents of warm air that paved the path to its secret home.

After a while, Bridie has the idea to try a new tactic. She puts on her most hurt expression, and tries to look close to tears. 'It's true,' she tells Doctor Joseph. 'Really it is. She said nothing more that I can remember.'

Perhaps because he is taken in and feels he has gained some advantage, sensing that his patient is finally weakening, the doctor presses on. 'You're a very bright and intelligent girl, Bridie,' he declares in a matter-of-fact way, 'and I just cannot bring myself to believe that you smothered your baby brother simply because this lady friend of yours said it was expedient. She must have said something more to make you do it. Or,' he adds, pronouncing the words like an accusation, 'you had reasons of your own for killing him.'

Bridie's attitude changes immediately. She looks furious, and when she replies her voice is cold and hard and aloof. 'Well, Joseph,' she says, stressing his name and thus making it almost derogatory, 'if you don't believe what I tell you there's really no point in my telling you anything, is there?'

'As long as you tell me the truth, Bridie, I –'

'I *am* telling you the truth.'

'All of it?'

'Yes.'

Bridie watches as the doctor puts a big question mark after what he has written on his silly pad, and she finds this amusing. She smiles surreptitiously, and is still smiling to herself when the doctor looks up, and says: 'Well, let's leave that for a moment and move on to something else. Tell me instead what you felt.'

'About what?' Bridie demands, determined to teach him a lesson by being difficult.

'When you realised you had actually killed Oliver – what did you feel? Were you shocked, or sorry, or frightened, or what?'

Careful now, Bridie, never rush into anything. 'I don't think I had any particular feeling,' Bridie admits after a while.

Doctor Joseph makes it very clear that there is no way he is going to accept that. He snorts. 'Oh come on now, Bridie. You don't really expect me to believe that. You must have had *some* feeling,' he insists.

'No,' Bridie tells him seriously. 'I can't remember that I had.'

The doctor takes to shaking his head again, not this time, it appears, in disbelief, but in cold astonishment. And, feeling suddenly generous, Bridie gives him an encouraging grin.

'I just smothered him and went back to my bed and fell sound asleep,' she says.

'You just smothered your brother and went back to your bed and fell sound asleep,' the doctor repeats word for word as though trying to impress the grim, uncaring sequence on his brain.

'That's right.'

'You actually slept?'

'Of course. I was very tired.'

Shortly after the Silver Lady had collected her shadow and flown from the room, Bridie threw back the blankets and jumped from her bed. For some moments she just stood there, her head cocked to one side as though listening, frowning as if what she heard was difficult to comprehend. Then slowly, almost imperceptibly, she began to smile, her eyes becoming strangely opaque, her fingers clutching at something only she could visualise. On tiptoe she left her room and crept down the passageway to the nursery – a small, beamed room that Mummy had adorned with mobiles. She hesitated at the door, listening to Mummy snore softly in the next room, and then went in, closing the door carefully, noiselessly behind her. She stole her way to the cot in the corner, stopping once and sucking in her breath as one of the glass mobiles tinkled. She leaned over and peered at her sleeping brother. He looked very peaceful, lying on his back, his face, in repose, like that of an old man, unlined, of course, but seeming infinitely wise. He made little sucking noises with his mouth, both his hands clasped into fists.

Bridie leaned down and placed one hand under his head,

raising it: with her other hand she eased out the pillow from under it. Oliver did not stir: sleeping blissfully he gave a small cough and gurgled, even showing a glimmer of a smile. Bridie clutched the pillow to her chest, and gazed down on him fondly. Then, still with fondness as her expression, she placed the pillow over Oliver's face and held it there.

– Dreadful, Mrs Canty called it, stressing her feelings by shaking her head. That poor woman. Quite dreadful.

– Careless, I call it, Miss Calilly called it. Cot-death indeed! As fancy a name as you like for sheer carelessness. The baby wasn't put down right, that's all.

– Whatever – Mrs Canty began.

– All this stupid pampering, Miss Calilly interrupted. On its back it should have been, and with no pillow. All that ridiculous, namby-pamby soft bedding – of course it was going to suffocate.

– It's still a dreadful thing to have happened.

– That's as may be, but she'll have no sympathy of mine.

– I don't expect it's sympathy she'll be wanting, Mrs Canty countered, and then frowned, wondering what it was one wanted on such dreadful occasions.

Oliver barely resisted: his tiny fingers with their little pink nails cluched at the air briefly, and he kicked a few times but that was all. Bridie was surprised. Not that she had given much thought as to what she might expect, but there should, she felt, have been some rather more dramatic climax to her monstrous actions. Even when she eventually removed the pillow and gazed into the cot it was anti-climactic: Oliver might simply have been continuing his untrammelled sleep. There was no sign of the blueness she had imagined suffocation would bring; there was no sign on the baby's face that he had experienced a brutal, premature end. And he was still warm: Bridie had expected him to go cold and rigid immediately. She wondered if he was really dead. To be sure she placed the pillow over his face again, and as she held it there, pressing it down, she recited a nursery rhyme. Humpty Dumpty sat on a wall, she whispered. Humpty Dumpty had a great fall. Silly, stupid Humpty Dumpty. He should have known better. Just like Oliver should have known better than to get in the way, to come between her and Mummy. Just like Mummy should have known better than to be so unkind to Daddy and send him away. Well, Oliver wouldn't get in the way any more, and as for Mummy . . .

Bridie removed the pillow and carefully placed it back under Oliver's head. He was getting cold now, she noted, and stiff, and his colour was grey, not blue. Bridie turned him over, leaving him face down. Then she kissed the back of his head, and went back to bed. In no time at all she fell asleep.

It was Mummy screaming that woke her up with a start. She took her time getting out of bed, carefully putting on her slippers and dressing-gown (the pretty quilted dressing-gown that Daddy had given her, saying: That's for you, my lovely) before trotting along to the nusery to study the result of her atrocity.

'Well, when you woke up in the morning,' Doctor Joseph persists, recovering his calm composure and determined to force Bridie into telling him something significant, something that would give him an inkling as to the reason behind her action. 'In the morning – what did you feel?'

Bridie screws up her face into defiant lines: she is equally determined to keep the doctor guessing: why should he get the answer to something she really does not fully understand herself? 'I don't remember that either,' she says.

'Try and remember,' the doctor orders.

Bridie starts to enjoy herself, putting on expressions that might indicate she is trying desperately to remember what the doctor finds so vital. 'I'm so sorry, Doctor Joseph,' she says finally, even her smile apologetic. 'But I'm a complete blank,' she adds innocently and is agreeably surprised when the doctor surrenders and seems to accept her blankness as a possibility.

'You remember nothing,' he says, making it a statement.

'I remember Mummy screaming her head off,' Bridie informs him enthusiastically. 'That's what woke me up, I think. Mummy and her screaming.'

'And when you heard that, what did you do?'

'I got out of bed,' Bridie says, speaking very slowly and using her fingers to numerate her actions, bending one forward as each was eliminated. 'Then I put on my slippers and dressing-gown – the one Daddy gave me. Then I went down the passage to the nursery – that's where Mummy was. Screaming.'

'Then what?'

'I comforted Mummy, of course.'

'How did you do that?'

'The same way everyone comforts people,' Bridie replies grandly.

Mummy was holding the stiff little corpse in her arms, wailing. She was rocking it to and fro as though Oliver had just fallen asleep after lengthy persuasion and she wanted to make certain he stayed that way. Her eyes were open and looked wild and a bit crazy. With her face still showing traces of last night's cleansing cream and her unbuttoned, kimono-like dressing-gown slipping from one shoulder, her bare toes curling in and out on the carpet like clutching, stubby fingers and her hair uncombed and dishevelled, she looked like a witch Bridie had seen portrayed in a book somewhere. Even the thin band of ribbon she used to tie her hair at night had unravelled and hung down her back, giving its own untidy madness to the scene. Bridie walked silently across the room until she was directly in front of her mother, and then stood there, observing the ritual of mourning.

– What's the matter, Mummy? she asked when she had seen enough to satisfy her curiosity.

– Oh, Bridie, Bridie, Mummy moaned, still using her high-pitched, wailing voice.

– Whatever is the matter, Mummy? Bridie asked again.

– It's our baby, Mummy whispered, using the plural for reasons known only to herself, and placing Oliver back in his cot, even covering him up as though suspecting he might catch a chill, before turning and falling on her knees, clutching Bridie to her. Oliver is dead, she announced bluntly into Bridie's neck.

– Oh dear, Bridie said. Then, deciding this was hardly enough: How terrible, she added.

Mummy didn't hear her, of course, she was too busy snivelling on her shoulder, making Bridie smile as she exclaimed over and over through her sadness: You poor darling, Bridie. I'm so sorry. What a shock for you. You poor darling. I *am* sorry. Bridie stroked her mother's tangled hair.

– I shouldn't have told you just like that, Mummy apologised. Did I frighten you?

– A little, Bridie lied, glad to bleed what compassion she could from the circumstance, now running her fingers through the strands of Mummy's hair and disentangling them like she was combing them.

– Forgive me, darling, will you? Mummy begged, holding Bridie's face between her hands and kissing it all over.

– Of course, Mummy, Bridie forgave, and pulled herself free, making for the cot. Are you sure he's dead?

– Yes, dear, Mummy confirmed, sitting back on her hunkers and looking pretty pathetic.

Bridie felt Oliver's hand. He *is* cold, isn't he? she remarked.

That set Mummy off again, sobbing and choking and sniffing. It started her talking to herself too. What do I do? she wanted to know. What on earth do I do? Who do I tell?

– The police, I suppose, Bridie told her.

– The police? Mummy sounded horrified.

– I suppose so. Don't you have to call the police when there's a mysterious death?

Mysterious death? Mummy repeated vaguely.

– And the doctor, Bridie went on. The doctor first, I should think. To determine cause, she explained, remembering the expression from some television programme.

Mummy crawled across the floor, looking ridiculous, and started hugging Bridie again. Of course, she said. Of course you're quite right, Bridie. Whatever would I do without you?

Bridie freed herself from Mummy's grip again and pulled the kimono properly into place. The best thing is, she said, that you go and telephone the doctor and then go and get dressed. And I'll make you a cup of tea. It will all seem better after you've had a cup of tea, Bridie prognosed, remembering Granny always maintained that a cup of tea shed a different light on problems.

– Oh, Bridie, you are an angel.

It proved to be a momentous day. The doctor came and examined Oliver, at one stage holding him up to the light as though to look through him. Then he took Mummy by the arm and led her away from the nursery, taking her into her bedroom and making her sit down. He looked very morose and solemn as he talked to her, and his concern set Mummy crying again.

– It's one of those inexplicable tragedies, Bridie heard him say. Nobody is to blame. God wanted your child and took him, he added, perhaps feeling a touch of the occult would go down well with the distraught woman. And there's no need to call the police, he went on. It's what we call a natural death and I will report it as such.

– Thank you, doctor, Mummy thanked him, gulping the words. I'm sorry I'm so –

– I'll leave you these, the doctor interrupted, taking a small bottle of pills from his old-fashioned, battered, Gladstone bag and putting them on the table beside the bed. Take two before you go to bed tonight, he told her. Just two, mind, and that will give you a good night's sleep. And if you need me you only have to call, he concluded kindly.

All those pills seemed to do, however, was make Mummy more maudlin, and it struck Bridie that from the time the doctor left to the day of the funeral Mummy spent her time perpetually in a state of tears. She was worst on the morning of the burial: the steady stream of tears eating into the make-up she applied to her cheeks with such urgency, making sinister lines on her face. More than once she reapplied it, thicker each time as though it was a sort of memorial to her child. You're so strong, Bridie, she remarked once between applications. I wish I was as strong as you.

– I'm trying to be, Mummy, Bridie replied. I have to be strong and look after you. But really I'm crying too. Inside. I'm crying inside, she said, and liked the sound of that very much, so she repeated it: Really crying inside.

Mummy liked the sound of it too, gazing at Bridie in haunted admiration. Oh, Bridie, she said. My darling little Bridie. You're all the world to me now.

– And you're all the world to me, Mummy, Bridie replied as though meaning it, smiling inside herself as she watched Mummy's face go all grateful and lovey.

– We'll survive all this together, won't we, darling?

– Of course we will, Mummy.

'How did you comfort her – your mother?' Doctor Joseph asks as if anticipating an intriguing reply.

Bridie puts on her prim face. 'It was really very difficult,' she says. 'Mummy went completely to pieces. Crying all the time. I had to do everything.'

'But you must have felt sorry for her.'

'Yes and no.'

The doctor waits for an elaboration of this.

'It was very difficult to feel really sorry for her. I mean, there was no need for her to go on and on the way she did,' Bridie says, sounding severe as a matron.

'It doesn't sound as though you comforted her very well,' the doctor observes, aware that this would antagonise her and getting ready to write down her reply.

'I most certainly did,' Bridie snaps, her eyes alight with anger. 'I did everything for her. I cooked and cleaned and made the beds. And I let her hang on to me at the funeral,' she concludes vehemently as if this had been her greatest contribution.

'That was the least you might have done,' Doctor Joseph says.

'What did you expect me to do?' Bridie counters, still very annoyed. 'How do you think I felt with Mummy hanging on to me and crying and all those people watching. I think it was very good of me to tolerate that.'

'Oh, you do?'

'Yes. I do. I could just as easily have stayed at home. In fact, Mummy said I should stay at home. I only went so that I could help her through the burial.'

And this was the truth: Kathleen Lynch did tell Bridie not to come to the graveyard, and she did hang on to her when she insisted on coming, squeezing her hand so tightly that it soon became numb. The burial was a dismal affair. It drizzled non-stop throughout the graveside ceremony adding a grim chillness to the melancholy scene, and the priest had to keep taking off his spectacles and wiping them, interrupting what he was saying, making the whole thing take twice as long as was necessary.

The whole village turned out, but respectfully kept their distance, huddling in groups some way from the grave, praying the responses and blessing themselves when the liturgy called for it. Away to the left, under the single tree that flourished in the small cemetery, a tree blackened by regular, fearsome attacks by lightning, the shaulies stood, not speaking, hoarse from their keening of the night before, waiting for payment, unable to collect their fee until the coffin had been lowered lest, by some awful error, the body within it still lived, and they would have to keen professionally again, offering a sort of ghastly refund. Last night their doleful dirge had terrified Kathleen Lynch, but Bridie had enjoyed it, and she had stayed up late listening, fantasising that the melodies of woe had the same mournful lilt as the vixen's wails of pain.

Then the little white coffin was lowered on white plastic ropes into the earth and someone threw some clay in on top of it when Mummy refused to, preferring to sob bitterly and call out Oliver's name in whispers.

And she was still sobbing intermittently as they walked back to the mill. They were the first to leave the cemetery, the villagers falling back while maintaining their ranks to form a corridor of steaming, damp bodies, Mummy with her head bent to her chest, Bridie holding her gloved hand and bowing solemnly in thanks to the women who smiled consolingly and to the men who doffed their hats and caps out of respect, all the while relishing the look in their eyes that told her she was a brave little girl, and a grand little child to look after her poor mother the way she was doing.

– There's only you and me now, Bridie, Mummy said that evening as they sat cuddled up in front of the fire that Bridie had insisted on lighting despite Mummy's typically illogical protestation that such comfort was indecent if Oliver wasn't there to share it.

– Yes, Bridie agreed.

– I'm so lucky to have you.

Bridie agreed with that too, but said nothing.

– I don't know how I would have managed without you, Mummy muttered, kissing the top of Bridie's head.

– Shush, Mummy, Bridie said.

– No, really, darling.

– Shush, Bridie told her again.

– First poor Charlotte and now Oliver. I'll die if anything happens to you, Mummy foretold, not thinking, and giving Bridie a hurried sideways glance in case she had frightened her.

She hadn't, of course. Nothing's going to happen to me, Bridie said.

– Of course it won't, Mummy said by way of reparation.

– It's you we have to think about, Mummy.

Mummy smiled and looked down at her fondly, holding her still tighter, her eyes filling with tears again. My darling Bridie, she said. I'll be all right. Give me a little time to get over the shock and then we can set about rebuilding our lives together.

– Yes, Bridie agreed.

– We will be happy, Mummy said in a fierce whisper.

– Of course we will. Oliver's death was sent to try us, Bridie said, remembering the phrase.

– Death is sent to try us, Mrs Lynch, the priest, Father Tierney, said in practised tones as though setting an examination. It is particularly difficult when a child is involved, he went on, perhaps to excuse Mummy's persistent crying. But we must always remember that God's ways are not our ways, he continued, warming up and falling automatically into the patter of his beliefs.

Not until the fire went out did they go to bed, Mummy wanting to stay awake as if sleep had suddenly become akin to death. Do you want to come and sleep with me in my bed tonight, Bridie? she asked.

Bridie shook her head. Not tonight, Mummy. I toss a lot, she explained. I'd keep you awake. You must be exhausted.

Mummy looked hurt for a moment but then she smiled again, and stroked Bridie's hand. You are such an angel, Bridie, she whispered. You're right. I am tired. Very tired.

– Of course you are. You take two of those tablets the doctor left you – just two, mind – and try and get a really good night's sleep.

– I will.

– And don't get up too early in the morning, Bridie ordered with mock severity. I'll bring you a nice cup of tea in bed and then you can get up nice and rested.

Mummy must literally have cried herself to sleep. From her room Bridie heard her sobbing and moaning away for hours until, suddenly, it all went quiet. Bridie was relieved at that: she was fully expecting the Silver Lady to visit again but suspected this was unlikely while Mummy kept up her silly racket.

Bridie notices that in a subtle way Doctor Joseph's attitude changes, and she doesn't like it one little bit. She decides she is going to be difficult, just to teach him a lesson. She listens to him recap the dialogue of the past few days but without looking at him, purposely avoiding his eyes each time he looks up as though for confirmation that he has overlooked nothing. She is delighted to note that this irritates him.

'Would you agree, Bridie, that that just about sums up what you have been telling me?' he asks at last, his irritation clipping his words, making them sharp and cross.

'Just about,' Bridie concedes, clipping her words too.

'Good. Then we can move on, can't we?'

Bridie gives him a stony look.

'Yes. I think we can,' the doctor thinks. 'Tell me, how soon after Oliver's death did your lady contact you again? The same day?'

'No.'

'Not the same day?'

'No.'

'When?'

'The night of the funeral,' Bridie says.

'Tell me about that visit,' the doctor says, adding please when he sees Bridie clamping her lips together firmly.

'What about it?'

'Was there anything different about it?'

'In what way?'

'In any way.'

Bridie closes her eyes pretending to think but getting ready to dash the doctor's hopes. 'No,' she tells him finally.

'I see,' Doctor Joseph says, and is about to make some more notes when Bridie interrupts him, giving a small, polite cough.

'Yes?' the doctor asks, looking up, although now with something like suspicion in his eyes.

'She was very pleased with me,' Bridie confides.

So is Doctor Joseph now, apparently. He turns the page of his notebook, giving himself plenty of room to write.

'Did she actually tell you that?' he asks.

'Yes.'

'Can you remember exactly what she said? The exact words?'

Bridie gives a deep sigh. 'I've told you before, doctor, she never spoke to me in words. She just put the thoughts of what she wanted to say into my head.'

'Ah, yes. So you did,' the doctor says, looking abashed and working his way back through his notes. 'She speaks to me from inside,' he reads and looks up. 'That's what you said.'

'Yes.'

'Well just to simplify things – for me, Bridie – can we just say she talked to you?'

'If you want.'

'Please.'

'Very well.'

'So,' the doctor repeats, grateful to have received one small concession, 'the night of Oliver's funeral she visited you and said she was very pleased with you?'

'That's right.'

'What else did she have to say?'

'Nothing.'

'Nothing at all?'

'No. Nothing at all,' Bridie lies, pleased with her morning's work.

Mummy could only have stopped sobbing a few minutes when the lady came and stood by Bridie's bed. She looked really lovely and, although there was no moonlight, her dress shimmered and shone and glimmered. Are you happy, Bridie? she asked.

– Oh yes, Bridie replied. Very happy.

– I'm so glad, the lady said.

– Not completely happy, Bridie heard herself say.

– I know. I know, the lady said kindly. But it is a beginning. From now on everything will move smoothly, but you must remember to take great care.

– Yes. I'll remember.

– And not be in a hurry. You must never rush headlong into anything, Bridie. You must always think first.

– Yes. I will.

– I will be on hand all the while to help you, but it is you alone who can make your life what you want it to be.

– Yes. I understand that.

– All I can do is guide you.

– Yes. Thank you.

Again the lady reached forward with both arms as though to embrace Bridie, but again she refrained, lowering her arms, then folding them. Do you love me, Bridie? she asked instead.

– Oh yes. Very much.

– You will never let anything come between us, will you?
– No. Never. I promise.
– You are my child, Bridie, and I am yours. We are one person, are we not?
Bridie glowed with delight. Oh yes.
– We must see to it that it remains so.
– Yes, indeed.
– I love you, my dear, dear, Bridie.
With that the lady was gone, not hurriedly but slowly fading into the darkness as though reluctant to withdraw. And it seemed to Bridie that there was something of her left behind: nothing tangible, of course, nor visible. Nothing that Bridie would ever be able to explain or share. What she left behind was a wonderful warmness that wrapped itself about Bridie like a mantle and made her strong and unafraid.

It was almost a week after the funeral that Bridie saw Mr Wyett again. She had called at his cottage a couple of times but he had been out both times: or seemed to be. Bridie thought she saw a curtain move the second time she visited but decided it must have been her imagination: Mr Wyett would hardly be avoiding her: he was her friend, was he not?
Yet when she finally caught him at home it struck her that Mr Wyett was unusually morose, his face quite grey and, uncharacteristically, unshaven. He welcomed her politely enough but there was almost a wariness in his eyes which was definitely odd, like he had been up to something he didn't want anyone to know about. Another thing: he didn't chatter in his usual way: he said nothing but Ah, good morning, Bridie, until they were both seated in his cluttered front room. And even when he got around to speaking and said: You must be very upset about your brother: his statement hinted there was more to it than one might at first suspect.
Bridie was hurt by this, and immediately went on her guard. Mummy is, she said, deflecting the upset.
– I'm sure. And you, Bridie?

– Oh yes. But not as much as Mummy. I didn't know him very well, you see.

Mr Wyett studied her face for a few moments before pointing out: He was your brother.

– Yes, I know, Bridie replied stiffly.

– You must miss him, Mr Wyett said, although, yet again, he seemed to be saying something else.

– Of course.

– Poor thing, Mr Wyett observed sadly, not making it altogether clear whether he meant Oliver or Bridie herself.

– Yes, Bridie agreed, but for some reason taking it that he had meant her mother. It means I have to look after her now.

– ?

– Mummy. I have to look after her.

– Oh. Yes.

– There's only me she can rely on now. Poor Mummy, she gets ever so addled when something unexpected happens. It was the same when Charlotte died. She went really strange for ages. I did tell you about Charlotte, didn't I?

Mr Wyett nodded. You did.

– To tell the truth, Daddy and I thought she was going mad. And it was the same again when Daddy left her. Not as bad as with Charlotte but queer enough I can tell you.

Mr Wyett continued to nod.

– Still, I expect we'll manage to make it through this as well, Bridie said brightly. It'll take her a while to get over the shock, I suppose, but she can lean on me again.

– Yes.

– Actually, Bridie went on, lowering her voice as if she was imparting a strict, adult confidence, I have to do almost everything now. Already. Mummy's still quite dazed, you know, and keeps forgetting to do things – simple, everyday things that *have* to be done. But she's getting better little by little which is good. It was just *awful* the morning she found Oliver.

– Your mother found him? Mr Wyett sounded surprised.

– Oh yes. I was fast asleep. It was her screaming that woke me up. It was *awful*, Mr Wyett, Bridie emphasised. Really awful.

There was simply nothing else she could think of to do. Kathleen Lynch clasped the dead baby to her and screamed. Yet, in a most peculiar way, the screaming was calculated, as though whatever mechanism in her head dealt with such horrors was selected and triggered as being the most effective to quell her agony once all more restrained reactions had been dismissed, as though only noise could master the searing pain. Oddly, it was a pain that seemed to be almost wholly physical, although this didn't occur to her until much later when she had the time to think about it rationally. The awful mental anguish which was supposed to accompany such incomprehensible tribulations was numbed by the appalling realisation of loss, and what she felt was a raging, unbearable turmoil in her stomach as though the child had, that minute, been ripped from her womb, leaving a gaping, bleeding wound that would never heal. True, something inside her head kept chipping away at her brain with cruel trickery, hinting at it all being an obscure punishment for some equally obscure malfeasance. Cackled accusations scampered across her mind as if it had suddenly become peopled by avenging demons hell-bent on imposing madness: and through it all one hard, unforgiving voice predominated, her mother's:

– What else did you expect, my girl, it said.

– I warned you, it said.

– God always punishes wickedness, it said.

– You can never flaunt in the face of God and expect to get away with it, it said.

– Always so quick to accuse others, it said.

– Always others in the wrong, never yourself, it said.

– The wrath of Almighty God is what you've invoked, Kathleen Lynch, it said.

– God giveth and God taketh away, it said.

– You should have learned your lesson when He took Charlotte, it said.

And so she screamed, clinging to the dead baby as though the warmth of her body might transmit life back to it. Oh, God, she screamed. Oh, God. Oh, God. Oh, God, she screamed over and over, each invocation a frightening damnation of this God who could be so cruel.

– My heart bled for you at the funeral, Mr Wyett was telling Bridie, somehow managing to nullify any melodramatics in the statement.

– Why? Bridie wanted to know.

– You looked so . . . Mr Wyett stopped, then tried again. You reminded me of . . . Once more he paused, floundering.

– Of what? Bridie asked, her interest heightened.

Mr Wyett opened his mouth to respond, but immediately snapped it shut again. He got cumbersomely to his feet and arched his back as though to relieve a nagging pain. He walked to the latticed window and stared out at the impending dusk, holding his waist, thumbs to the front, rocking on the balls of his feet. Then he came back across the room and gazed down at Bridie, his mournful eyes smeared with worry and contrasting sharply with Bridie's which, filled with curiosity, danced and sparkled like a meerkat's. Of someone I once knew, he said finally, but quietly, rather as if he was still trying to pull his reminiscence into focus.

– Oh? Who?

– Or maybe I never knew . . . Mr Wyett went on vaguely.

– You're terrible, Mr Wyett, Bridie announced, smiling pleasantly. You're always doing that to me, she said and gave a little frown at the familiarity of her statement. Daddy used to do it too. Start to say something really interesting and then stop dead just as he came to the best part. I *hate* that.

Mr Wyett looked appropriately chastened. I apologise, he apologised. It's just that there are some things that cannot be easily put into words.

Bridie nodded willingly. Yes, she agreed. I know that. I think that's why my Silver Lady never uses words. They're so very *restricting*, don't you think? she asked, obviously proud of her choice of word.

– Very, Mr Wyett heard himself say, taking Bridie's satisfied look to mean something else, and asking: You still see her?

– Lady? Of course. She's my very best friend.

Mr Wyett went back to his chair and sat down heavily. I thought I was, he said, half mockingly.

– You're different, Mr Wyett. You're my best *real* friend.

– Thank you.

Bridie beamed, and gave him a loving look.

– You don't think it strange that you have such a – such a close friendship with . . .

– With Lady? Bridie interrupted. Oh no. Do you?

Mr Wyett nodded. A little.

Bridie looked suddenly suspicious. Why?

Mr Wyett grimaced. I worry, he said, ignoring the question, glancing towards the succubus hanging over the fireplace.

– Why? Bridie asked again, now questioning his latest statement, she, too, looking at the grotesque figure in the picture.

– Because sometimes we lose control of them. Sometimes we let them demolish our identity.

Bridie frowned.

– It happens mostly to lonely people, Ignatious went on, his eyes closed. They withdraw from themselves, creating another person who thinks for them. They get drawn into an unfathomable communion with the unknown, and what they thought was unbelievable becomes credible, warped solutions pattering through the mind with damning simplicity. You don't understand, do you? he asked suddenly. Never mind. He stood up again and started pacing the room. Tell me, Bridie, did she – your friend – did she ever touch you?

– That's the second time you've asked me that, Bridie pointed out. No. I thought she was going to but she didn't.

– Ah.

– Why?

– Touch afrights me as a serpent's sting, Mr Wyett quoted mysteriously. He stopped pacing and stood beside Bridie looking down at her. Bridie, he said, I am your friend, you know.

Bridie smiled up at him. Yes, I know.

– And I would never harm or betray you.

Bridie stopped smiling. She looked away, but immediately looked back again, staring hard into Mr Wyett's face, her eyes taking on a brittle, angry glint. Something warned her that Mr Wyett was leading up to something, something unpleasant, something she did not want to hear.

– If I ask you one more question, will you answer me truthfully?

– Yes, Bridie said at once. Of course.

– Did you have anything to do with your brother's death?

Bridie's expression changed slowly. The anger disappeared, replaced by a look of great hurt. She shook her head. No, she whispered.

– And that is the absolute truth?

– Yes.

· THREE ·

THE DOCTOR SEEMS pretty brusque this morning, probably for the benefit of the other man he has brought with him. 'Bridie,' he says, 'this is Mr Masterson. He's going to help us from now on.'

Bridie inclines her head, smiling to herself: she recognises the man as a policeman, one of the many who had come to the mill: he wore the same tie then, and Bridie remembers it. 'Is he a doctor too?'

'A specialist,' the doctor says.

'Oh. In what?'

'In life,' Mr Masterson puts in.

'That's nice,' Bridie tells him, already preparing to keep an eye on him, and bamboozle him if she could.

The doctor coughs, clearing his throat.

Bridie settles herself on her chair, looking pert.

Mr Masterson sits behind the doctor, crossing his legs.

'Today,' the doctor begins, starting a clean, white page of his silly notebook, and looking very determined, 'I want to talk about Miss Calilly.'

'All right,' Bridie agrees willingly, leaning forward a little as if she is going to deal with this matter earnestly.

'Can you tell me why you hated her so much?'

Bridie looks surprised. 'I didn't *hate* her.'

'But you did kill her –'

Bridie nodded. 'Yes. But I didn't *hate* her. I felt quite sorry for her really.'

'Then why did you murder her?' Mr Masterson interjects quickly, immediately wilting under the doctor's testy glare.

'She was in the way,' Bridie explains obligingly.

'Of what, Bridie?' the doctor asks, coaxingly.

'Of our plan.'

'*Our* plan?'

'Yes. Mine and Lady's.'

'Ah,' the doctor sighs and scribbles something down. 'And what plan was that?'

Bridie stares blankly at the doctor for a few moments, then shifts her gaze to the policeman, noting with satisfaction the expectant light in his eyes, then back to the doctor again. She decides not to answer for the moment: leave them waiting.

Overnight, it seemed, summer arrived in the village. One night the buds were clamped tight against the cold; the next morning they burst wide open in the warmth of the sun. The trees waved their new-born, pale-green leaves like joyous bunting; flowers blossomed and filled the air with scent. Cattle lounged in the meadows, chewing, their tails flicking over their backs. The windows of the houses were thrown open now that the dejected spirits of winter no longer threatened. Curtains and heavy blankets were hung on lines; mats were beaten, and the chimney-sweep went from house to house, getting blacker and blacker, perhaps more and more lucky to the touch.

– Bridie, Mummy said, be an angel and run down to Mrs Canty's and get me a small bag of flour, will you. Self-raising. I thought I'd make us a cake for tea.

Kathleen Lynch watched Bridie walk down the path from the mill, swinging her little basket. She marvelled at how the girl had coped since Oliver's death, growing up, becoming so self-assured. A tower of strength, she told Granny on the telephone.

– And you? Granny asked, dutifully.

– Me? Oh I'm all right, mother.

– Not moping, I hope.

– No, I'm not moping. Lonely, but not moping.

– I saw Francis the other day, Granny put in, finding her cue in her daughter's admission of loneliness.

– Oh.

– He was asking for you.

– Oh.

– He'd like to see you again.

– I'm sure he would.

– He misses you, and Bridie.

Kathleen said nothing.

– You might have got in touch with him after the accident, Granny scolded.

– He was informed.

– Not by you.

– No. But he was told. He could have come to the funeral.

– He thought it better not to intrude.

– I'm sure.

– It's really not healthy you and Bridie living down there by yourselves.

Kathleen laughed. It's perfectly healthy, I assure you, mother.

– Bridie needs a father. You're simply being selfish.

– Maybe I'll get her one, Kathleen snapped, angry at the unjust accusation.

Yet Kathleen Lynch had often wondered if she was being selfish, if she was depriving Bridie by tucking her away in the country, imposing her own yearning for isolation on her child. But she had always, up until now, managed to defend her decision by clothing it in the respectability of 'protection'. She was shielding Bridie, she told herself, allowing her to develop in peaceful surroundings, giving her time to get over the damage her father might have inflicted on her mind. What matter that she herself felt abandoned and nightly sobbed herself to sleep, her body aching for the touch of someone who loved her? Frequently, more frequently since Oliver's death, she had taken to studying herself in the mirror, being objective. She was still attractive, was she not? Certainly. Still desirable, even at thirty-eight, her complexion smooth and unlined, her figure slim, Kathleen Lynch held the tempting quality of someone about to become beautiful, of someone who would blossom from a lover's embrace. But in a curious, stubborn way she got grim satisfaction from telling herself she was withholding her charms, keeping herself unsullied as a kind of retribution, although how long she could sustain her abstinence was anybody's guess. More than once she had contemplated inviting one of Francis's friends to visit for a weekend, justifying such action by seeing it as a suitable revenge on her husband. Indeed, she had even gone so far as to telephone Michael Petty (Francis's 'best' friend, who had made it clear he lusted after her, seeking out her company at parties, being overly jolly, making her 'one of the boys' which condoned a certain boisterousness and crudity) but had replaced the receiver as soon as he had answered.

Bridie took her time going to the shop, strolling down the village street. All about her, things bustled. Someone sang, someone whistled, pots rattled, the smell of jam being made oozed from a window, somewhere unseen two women chattered, their clacking like the sound of some exotic bird. Old people had taken to sitting on kitchen chairs in front of their homes, their dimming eyes squinting at what could be their last taste of summer, any summer, their frail bodies rigid as though they feared the sudden warmth could crack their brittle bones.

– Good morning, Bridie, Mrs Canty said.
– Good morning, Mrs Canty.
– And what can I do for you?
– Some flour. Self-raising. That's all, thank you.
– Baking today, are we?
– Mummy is. A cake, she said.

– A cake! Mrs Canty exclaimed as though a miracle might be in the offing.

– So she said.

– How lovely.

– Yes.

– You're both keeping well? Mrs Canty enquired, placing the bag of flour on the counter and plumping it up with both hands.

– Oh yes. Very well.

– Good. Everything seems better in the sunshine, don't you think?

– Yes.

The flour in her basket, Bridie set off for home. She thought about stopping to pay Mr Wyett a visit, was on the point of doing just that when she heard the voices. She stopped and listened. Behind the high hedge of Miss Calilly's cottage two women were chatting. One was Miss Calilly herself: Bridie recognised the nasal whine instantly. The other voice was new to her.

– . . . definitely wrong, Miss Calilly was saying.

– I don't see –

– I don't expect you do, Fiona. You're just like everyone else. You take everything the authorities say as gospel.

– They do *know* about such things.

– They *think* they know, you mean. You mark my words, there's more to that child's death than meets the eye. Cot-death, indeed!

– It does happen, Fiona whoever-she-was pointed out.

– Not in my book, Miss Calilly said. I always said there was something odd about that other child. The girl. Bridie. Far too sure of herself for her own good. Always in and out of that dreadful Mr Wyett's house. Always sneaking about. She's up to something, I tell you.

– Don't be silly.

– I'm not being silly, Miss Calilly protested. I can sense things. And I can tell you there's something uncanny about that child. The way she looks at you. Have you noticed that? No, of course you haven't. Like she didn't have to listen to what you were saying: like she knew what you were going to say even before you had thought of it yourself. And why is she always going off into those woods by herself? Answer me that.

– Why not? The woods are beautiful. I used to go there a lot when I was her age.

– Maybe you did. But you didn't go every day, hail, rain or snow. Always sneaking about. I tell you, Fiona, there's going to be more trouble from that quarter before very much longer.

Bridie moved along the hedge and peered over the gate.

– Oh. Bridie. Good morning, Miss Calilly said.

– Good morning, Miss Calilly.

– What are you up to this morning?

– Just shopping. Flour.

– Oh.

– Before I go to the woods.

– Oh.

– There's all sorts of things happening there now.

– Really?

– Oh yes.

– Like what?

– Things, Bridie said, deciding to be mysterious. Strange things, she added, trying to make her voice sound creepy.

– Indeed? Miss Calilly asked, and sniffed, giving her friend a knowing, sideways glance.

Bridie nodded.

– You'd be much better off in school instead of running wild about here, Miss Calilly pronounced.

– I'm going in September.

– High time too.

– Meanwhile, Bridie said, I do all my learning in the woods. You'd be surprised what you can hear if you listen.

– Would I, indeed.

Bridie nodded again. Yes. The trees are very old and wise, you know. They can tell you all sorts of things that you would never imagine.

Miss Calilly gave a small shudder.

– Anyway, I must be off, Bridie said cheerfully, and off she went, smiling to herself, wondering what Lady would have to say when she heard what Miss Calilly had been saying.

With no answer forthcoming the doctor decided to come directly to the main incident, perhaps nudged there by Mr Masterson's impatient fidgeting. 'When you killed Miss Calilly – was it a spur-of-the-moment act, or did you think about it for some time?'

'Oh, I never rush into anything, doctor,' Bridie answers. 'I always think about things very carefully.'

– Never rush into anything, Bridie, Lady warned.

'So you thought very carefully about the killing?'

'Oh yes. I had to talk the matter over with Lady, too. I mean, it's not the sort of thing you do lightly, is it?'

The doctor looks taken aback. 'No. It's not,' he agrees, clearly playing for time, wondering where to go from here. Then: 'You talked it over with Lady, you said?'

'That's right.'

'And whose decision was it in the end – to kill Miss Calilly, I mean?'

Bridie thinks for a moment. 'We both decided at the same time,' she says pensively. 'Yes, we both decided together.'

'Well did you *suggest* the actual killing or did Lady?'

Bridie thinks again, frowning. 'Oh dear,' she says, smiling disarmingly, putting on her regretful, innocent look. 'I can't honestly remember that,' she lies.

'Try,' Mr Masterson says coldly.

'Yes, try,' the doctor urges kindly.

Bridie pretends to try.

The woods are really lovely. The stark, gaunt, bareness of the cruel months was gone. The sun, filtering through the uppermost branches of the great trees, gave warmth to the earth that had been frozen, dormant, for so long, making everything lush and vibrant and cheerful; and Bridie felt that warmness wrap itself about her as she made her way to her secret place. As ever, she felt a wonderful peace descend upon her, lifting her spirit, making her weightless, as though she was nearing that region where timelessness began. The mosses and pine-needles and humus made the earth beneath her feet soft and spongy: she imagined she was gliding over the ground, not touching it, flying. And there was something more: it was as though her spirit, too, was flying, flying ahead of her, beckoning her forward, gliding gaily, laughing, hiding behind trees from time to time and suddenly jumping out as in a marvellously innocent game of hide-and-seek. And Bridie chased it, her own happy laughter echoing through the wood.

– I don't want to play that game, Bridie said.

– Oh, come on, Bridie Lynch. Don't be such a spoil-sport, Patricia Brazier said. It's only a game.

– I don't want to.

– Nothing *happens*, Patricia Brazier insisted. Nothing much, anyway. We just kiss, that's all.

– I don't want to kiss, Bridie insisted.

– I tell you what. You can have Peter. He's far the best-looking.

– I don't want Peter.

– Oh, come on.

– You go. Go by yourself. You don't need me.

–Oh, come on.

– No.

– Why not?

– I don't like it.

Patricia Brazier turned nasty. You like it well enough when your Daddy does it. That's what I hear.

– My Daddy loves me.

– Yeah. He really loves you all right. *My* Daddy says it's filthy what he does to you.

– You're horrible, Patricia Brazier, Bridie screamed. Your Daddy's a wicked liar and so are you.

Soon Bridie arrived at the massive tree where the old owl lived. It was very still and quiet. Nothing stirred. It was like a magic circle, Bridie decided, since outside the invisible boundary the activity continued: she could hear the birds singing and the small animals gibbering, but at a distance. Like being at mass, she thought: very awesome and attentive within the church, yet the sounds from outside penetrated, enhancing the sanctity somehow, making the church a special refuge. And so it was now: nothing could touch her here; nobody could tease or belittle her; everything protected her from all that was harsh and cruel and hurtful.

There was no sign of the owl, yet Bridie sensed it was nearby. Watching her, no doubt: watching *over* her, which was comforting. Bridie pressed her face against the rugged trunk of the owl's tree. Then she kissed it.

– Hello, Bridie.

Without hurrying, Bridie turned and smiled at her Silver Lady. Hello, she said.

– You look very pretty today, my dear. What a lovely summer dress you are wearing.

– Thank you.

– But you look sad, too, my child.

Bridie leaned her face against the tree again, and closed her eyes. Not sad, she said. Concerned.

– Ah.

– Upset.

– Ah. What has upset you?

– Something I heard this morning.

– Oh yes. That would be Miss Calilly.

– You know?

– Of course.

– Yes. Of course.

– You mustn't worry your pretty little head about that silly woman.

– She's wicked.

– Yes. Yes, she is, Lady agreed thoughtfully.

– She says horrible things.

– Yes.

– And she makes other people *think* horrible things.

Lady nodded.

– What can we do, Lady?

– What do you think we should do?
– We should stop her.
– Yes. But how?
– I've thought of a way.
– Are you sure?
– Oh, yes.
– And you've thought about it carefully?
– Yes.
– It will not bring you pain?
– No.
– Then you must do as you think best. I will take care of you. You know that.
– Yes. I know.

Bridie opened her eyes and found herself alone. She felt suddenly cold, and shuddered. She moved a few feet from the tree and hugged herself, listening. There was no sound. Everything was, it seemed, holding its breath as though, having eavesdropped, it was mulling over the consequences that might be forthcoming.

The doctor takes Mr Masterson out of the room, and returns alone a few minutes later. 'That's better,' he says to Bridie with a satisfied grin.

'Yes. Much,' Bridie agrees.

'Mr Masterson, I fear, is only interested in the mundane facts.'

Bridie shrugs. 'That's his job, isn't it? All the police ever want is the bare facts,' she says with a smug grin.

'Oh. You knew.'

'That he was a policeman? Of course.'

'How did you know that?' the doctor asks as though hoping he would get an unusual, revealing response.

'I'd seen him before.'

'Oh,' the doctor says, deflated.

Bridie giggles.

The doctor gives a small, embarrassed giggle too. 'Anyway, we seem to get on much better by ourselves, don't we?'

Bridie does not answer.

The doctor looks back through his notes, running his ball-point pen down the lines as he reads them, mouthing the words silently. 'So,' he continues finally, 'you made a plan with Lady and decided that Miss Calilly had to be killed?'

'Yes.'

'Did you have to *kill* her, Bridie, I mean, wasn't there some other way you could – what? – punish her? Frighten her, perhaps?'

'She was wicked.'

'Even so –'

'Killing her was the only way.'

'Tell me – did you enjoy killing her?'

Bridie looks puzzled. 'Enjoy it?' she asks. 'No. I didn't *enjoy* it. I just did it.'

'Did you feel sorry afterwards?'

Now Bridie looks surprised. 'No. Why should I?'

'I think most people would feel some remorse.'

Bridie ignores that.

'It's a pretty terrible thing to kill another person, isn't it?'

Bridie ignores that too.

'You must have had *some* feelings about it.'

Bridie thinks about that. 'No. I don't think so. At least I don't remember having any. I just killed her and that was that.'

Doctor Joseph feels he should write that down, and he writes it down carefully, adding a full stop with a flourish. 'So, you simply waited for her to come along and then you pushed her off her bicycle. She hit her head on a stone. And that was it?'

'Yes,' Bridie lies.

'Then you ran back to the village and told Mrs Canty that there had been an accident?'

'Yes.'

The doctor shakes his head in wonderment. 'As simple as that?'

'Yes.'

'Amazing.'

'Yes, it was amazing really.'

And in a sense it was, if only for its simplicity. Everything fell into place so nicely that Bridie suspected Lady had taken a hand in it.

It was Friday afternoon, a bit cloudy but warm and pleasant for all that. Thunder had been forecast but it never came. Bridie had decided to forego her daily visit to the woods, and had crossed the stream and walked out into the countryside where the meadows seemed greener and the earth less unrewarding. Why she had made this decision was something she could never explain: it simply seemed the right thing to do. She stayed on the track, following it as it rose steeply from the valley. At the top she rested, sitting on the low, stone wall, sucking the sweet juice from a long and succulent blade of grass. She could clearly see the track stretch away from her on either side, towards the next village on her left, towards home on her right. She had been there some time, was even thinking it was time to go, when she spotted Miss Calilly pedalling towards her, returning, Bridie supposed, from visiting her married sister which she did every week, the two of them sharing the gossip from either village. Bridie watched. She saw Miss Calilly dismount at the foot of the hill, saw her lift her yapping terrier from the basket on the handlebars and set it on the ground, saw her lean forward and start pushing her bicycle up the incline. Miss Calilly didn't look up: she kept her head bent and trudged along, picking her way.

Bridie felt herself tingle. She jumped from the wall and raced down the hill towards home. At the bottom she hid herself behind the gnarled stump of a dead elm, peeping out to survey the brow of the hill, waiting for Miss Calilly to appear. It took ages and ages. Then suddenly, she was there, resting a moment, before returning her dog to the basket and getting on her bicycle, free-wheeling down the hill, going nicely fast, seeming, almost, to be enjoying it. Bridie started to shake. She crouched, both hands on the ground in front of her, ready to spring. She heard the metallic rattles of the protesting mudguards. She heard a shrill yap from the little dog. She heard the bell ping as the clapper was jostled against the shell each time the bicycle hit a rutty bump. She heard, she fancied, Miss Calilly's heavy breathing.

Patiently Bridie waited until the woman had passed her, then she sprang out. She raced after the bicycle and pushed Miss Calilly from it as hard as she could, watching her hurtle through the air and slam into the hard stone wall, and lie there, moaning, twitching, her mean little eyes wide open but unseeing, rolling a bit.

Bridie stood over her, studying her, waiting for her to die. But she wasn't going to die, it seemed. Not for a while anyway. She continued to moan but appeared to be recovering. Her eyes stopped rolling and focused on Bridie, at first bewildered but slowly filling with awareness and hate. Bridie sighed and moved to the wall, selecting the biggest stone she could lift. She raised it, held it aloft for a few seconds, studying Miss Calilly's eyes as the hatred changed to horror, then smashed it down on her head.

'And everyone believed you?' Doctor Joseph asks, still with lingering amazement in his voice.

Bridie smiles charmingly. 'Of course,' she says, then frowns.

'You look as though you're not so sure.'

'Well, the Inspector thought there was something a bit funny about the accident, but he believed me. He thought someone else might have killed her, I think.'

'But he believed you?'

'Yes.'

'And so did everyone else?'

Again Bridie hesitated. 'Yes.'

'You're sure?'

'I'm sure.'

– Mrs Canty, quick, there's been a terrible accident. I think Miss Calilly's been hit by a car. She's lying on the road just at the bottom of the hill. I think she's dead.

Bridie had purposely run all the way back to the village, her panting giving credence to her anxiety.

– Oh, dear Lord, Mrs Canty said, already out from behind the counter and making for the door.

– It's awful, Mrs Canty. Blood all over her, Bridie said.

Mrs Canty looked sick.

– Really awful, Bridie insisted.

Mrs Canty pulled herself together. Bridie, you run home and ask your Mummy to telephone the police, will you? And the doctor. Doctor Murray. Please.

– Yes, Mrs Canty. But I think it's too late for Dr Murray.

– You didn't see any sign of a car, did you? the Inspector asked Bridie later that evening.

– No.

– But you told Mrs Canty that you thought Miss Calilly had been hit by a car?

– Yes.

– What made you say that?

– I just *supposed* she must have been.

– She could have just fallen off her bike.

– Yes. But . . . Bridie stopped talking.

– But what? the Inspector urged.

Bridie gave a nervous little laugh. There was so much blood, Inspector. I thought there was too much blood if she had simply fallen off.

– When you found her – was she dead?

– I don't know. I didn't really look. I was so frightened I just ran all the way back to tell someone.

– And you saw nobody else near the area?

– No. Bridie shook her head.

– And you passed no one on the way home?

– No. But I wasn't really looking, you see. I just ran and ran as fast as I could.

– By the way – what were *you* doing out there?

– Me? Just walking.

– I don't like it, Bridie heard the Inspector remark to Doctor Murray. He had left the door ajar when he went to get Bridie's statement typed up. Something's wrong. Even the girl, Bridie

Lynch, said there was too much blood for someone just falling off a bike.

Doctor Murray sucked on his pipe for a moment. He was unaccustomed to violent death and was wary of it, approaching it cautiously as if it were a foreign disease. From force of habit he sought a simple explanation. Using his pipe he drew a small diagram in the air. She could have fallen off, he said, and that large stone could have toppled from the wall, striking her on the head.

– Could have.

– Could have.

– I still don't like it, the Inspector said.

– Well, there's only one alternative.

– I know.

– Either she fell off or someone killed her, the doctor pointed out.

– Yes. I know.

Doctor Murray allowed himself a small chuckle. I wouldn't try and read anything too sinister into it, Inspector.

The Inspector chuckled too. Perhaps you're right. You're satisfied it could have been an accident?

– I'd say it *was* an accident.

– I hope you're right.

– That Inspector thinks someone murdered Miss Calilly, Bridie told her mother that evening.

– Don't be silly, darling, Mummy replied. Nobody would murder Miss Calilly.

– The Inspector thinks someone did.

– He's got to think that. He's paid to be suspicious. He has to think of all the possibilities. You wait and see. In a few days it will be put down as the accident it was.

– That's what Doctor Murray says.

– There you are then.

– But the Inspector –

– If Doctor Murray says it was an accident you can be quite sure it was an accident. He'd know that sort of thing. Murder indeed! Really, Bridie. I am surprised. I never thought you'd be so very morbid.

And sure enough they called it an accident, or rather, death by misadventure, which Bridie thought was very grand. And everyone was very kind to her for a while, helping her through the shock of finding the body, although some of the older people eyed her curiously: twice, now, she had been close to unexpected death and perhaps they feared there was a hex about her. Some people, they knew, carried the power of death inside them, storing it in their souls until God wanted to use it.

Not that Bridie cared what anyone thought. Within days she had forgotten about Miss Calilly; forgotten, too, that she had been any part of her demise.

'I think,' Doctor Joseph says, smiling encouragingly, 'that you're telling me a bit of a fib.'

Bridie stares at him blankly.

'There was someone who didn't believe you – am I right?'

'You mean the Inspector? He did believe me. He thought there was something a bit odd all right, but he believed me just the same.'

'I didn't mean the Inspector.'

'Who?'

'That's what I want you to tell me, Bridie.'

'Everyone else believed me,' Bridie said, getting annoyed.

'You're quite certain?'

'Positive. Why should I lie to you?'

'Why indeed?'

As soon as she had finished telling Mr Wyett about the incident, Bridie knew he didn't believe her.

– I see, he said. That must have been terrible for you.

– Oh, it was, Mr Wyett. I was ever so scared.

– I'm sure.

– Why do you look at me like that?

– ? Like what, Bridie?

– Like you were laughing at me.

Mr Wyett shook his head, his expression filled with gloom. No, I'm certainly not laughing at you. Far from it, I'm afraid, he told her sadly.

– Well, it looked to me as if you were.

– So many things look differently to the way they really are. You should know that, Bridie.

– You're talking in those riddles again, Mr Wyett, Bridie said, wagging a finger mockingly, trying to make light of the conversation that had, without warning, become filled with a strange foreboding.

– Life is a riddle, child. As is death, alas.

Suddenly Ignatious Wyett swung away from her and strode to the window. It was already growing dark. He could hear a bird sing: a plaintive song: a sauley mourning the parting of the day. Moving his head slightly he caught a glimpse of his reflection in the window and, shuddering involuntarily, contemplated death staring him in the face. Not a pretty sight. Far away, beyond what now appeared to be his own contorted death-mask, beyond his neat, weedless garden, beyond the small fields and the woods, he witnessed the re-enactment of an extraordinary drama performed years ago; again it held frightening significance.

(Night. Bodies cluttering the floor their features dissembling always, finally, becoming ghastly caricatures of his dissimulating self: hell, a place more dead than death itself. Yes, most definitely hell, a horrible vision of hell brought about by his absurd dabbling in daemonic rituals. Yet, appallingly, he felt at home there, felt a kinship with the writhing corpses. The stench of evil ripped at his stomach. Screams like uncontrollable laments buffeted his consciousness. Then, abruptly, everything was still and silent. The bodies that had but a moment before been twisting in grotesque agony stood erect and beckoned to him. Their features were unblemished and beautiful, the festering wounds that had blighted them miraculously wiped away. They moved slowly towards him, calling his name. And they smiled, coming ever closer, surrounding him. They reached out as though to touch him, to caress him, to embrace him. Yet he felt cold, his mind chilled by an evilness he could not comprehend. Still they reached out but with urgency now. 'Oh God,' he screamed, and the spirits of the dead froze.)

– I don't know what you mean by that, Mr Wyett, Bridie said.

Mr Wyett turned from the window and walked back across the room. He seemed suddenly to have aged, his face ashen, his shoulders slumped. Don't you, Bridie?

– No, I don't.

Mr Wyett looked infinitely sad. No, he said. Perhaps you don't. Or perhaps you do but can't recognise it.

– Recognise what, Mr Wyett?

– Bridie – Mr Wyett began, pulling up a small chair and sitting down beside her. Tell me – please – the truth, I beg you – tell me, did you have anything to do with Miss Calilly's death?

Slowly Bridie turned and faced him, her face serious, her eyes sincere. No, she answered quietly.

Mr Wyett shook his head.

– You don't believe me, do you? Bridie asked.

– No, Bridie. I'm afraid I don't.

– I think you're horrible, Bridie snapped and stood up.

– Bridie, Bridie, Bridie. Sit down. Sit down – please.

Bridie sat down.

– I'm trying to help you. Believe me – all I want to do is help you. There are things that happen to us that we cannot understand. Events that overtake us. We do things as if we had no control over our actions, as if it is someone else inside us who is making us act. Often, once we have done something, we forget that we have done it. We can stand aloof and blame someone else. Do you understand me, Bridie?

Bridie didn't like the way the conversation was going. She didn't like it one little bit. Yet it fascinated her, and she nodded, folding her hands, preparing to listen to the end.

– Did your friend, the Silver Lady, put you up to it?

– To what?

– Bridie –

– I told you I had nothing to do with it.

Mr Wyett sighed. Have you seen your Lady recently?

– Yes. Of course. She's my friend.

– You saw her just before Miss Calilly was killed, didn't you?

Bridie shrugged. I might have done. I see her almost every day, you know.

– Does she ever put . . . put wicked thoughts into your head?

– Certainly not.

– And she has never touched you?

– Every time I see you you ask me that. No, she never touches me.

– I want to meet her, Bridie.

Bridie looked startled. She certainly hadn't expected that. Why?

– Can you arrange it?

– Why do you want to meet her? Bridie asked again.

– It's important that I do. Believe me.

– You'll frighten her away. You'll say something horrible to her and she'll never come to see me again.

– I won't say anything that will frighten her away. I promise. I just want to meet her, ask her a few questions. What harm can there be in that?

Bridie shrugged. None, I suppose.

– Well, then?

– I'll ask her if she wants to meet you. If she doesn't there's nothing I can do about it.

– I know that, Bridie.

– She's very fussy about who she meets.

– They usually are.

– Who?

– Our friends, Mr Wyett said. Those who pretend to guide us.

– All right, Bridie said. I'll ask her the next time I see her.

– Thank you.

– I'm not promising she'll meet you, mind. I'll just ask her and then it's up to her.

– I know. Thank you.

Alone, Ignatious Wyett sat huddled in his chair. He had been there since Bridie left a couple of hours earlier. He had not moved. Once he had moaned quietly to himself, and once he had muttered some words aloud. When he finally stood up and stretched himself, he was surprised to find himself crying.

– You look worn out, darling, Mummy said, when she got home from visiting Mr Wyett.

Bridie smiled. I *am* tired, Mummy.

– My poor baby. You've had a terrible time. Come over here to me.

Bridie went over to her mother and suffered her tender hugging. Mummy?

– Yes, darling?

– You know Mr Wyett?

– Yes.

– Do you think he's a nice man?

– I'm sure he is. Why?

– I just wondered.

Kathleen Lynch felt herself stiffen. She held Bridie at arm's length and looked at her severely. You must have had a reason for asking, she said.

– No, Bridie said vaguely.

– He's always nice to you, isn't he?

– Yes.

– He hasn't . . . Kathleen stopped, fumbling in her mind for the words she wanted.

– Hasn't what, Mummy?

– He hasn't touched you or anything, has he?

Bridie pulled herself away, and scowled. That's what he's always asking.

Kathleen looked puzzled. What?

– About Lady.

– What about Lady, Bridie?

– He's always asking if she touched me.

Kathleen felt relief sweep over her. She gave a small grateful laugh. You and your Lady, Bridie. A fine pair. Mr Wyett must be as silly as you are, asking if she touches you.

– He always asks that.

– And does she?

– No. Never. Neither does he. He wouldn't even shake hands with me.

– Why ever not?

– *I* don't know. He said touch frightened him like a snake.

– Frightened him like a snake? I never heard such rubbish. I expect he's a bit dotty, darling. Old men get dotty when they live on their own.

– Hmm. Yes. I expect that's it.

– I'm sure it is. Anyway, it's high time you were in bed.

– Yes. Yes it is.

In bed, warm and snug, Bridie waited. Lady would know what to do about Mr Wyett. She would soon sort things out.

Kathleen Lynch, also, waited. She waited for sleep to come. Recently, and for no definable reason, it had become a constant battle: it was as though every niggling worry and doubt, every problem, every yearning piled up to a massive accumulation during the day and exploded in her brain the moment her head touched the pillow. Then, too, there was the constant loneliness, the aching. Had she been in the city still, that could have easily been remedied. Indeed, she had tried it once, several weeks after Francis had packed his bags and crept off into the night. It had been a pretty lamentable exercise however, one that left her more bereft than before, and feeling sullied. And its failure to be anything more than a sexual romp had been entirely her own fault. She was prepared to admit this. He – one Denis Cannon, met during the interval after the first act of *Tosca*, and lulled by the promise of untold pleasures over a glass of tepid wine – had tried his best to be suitably enthusiastic. 'I could eat you,' he told her hungrily, eagerly stripping to his underwear and joining her in bed with a tremendous leap. The trouble was, when he had finished the main course and hygienically made for the bathroom, Kathleen Lynch felt nothing but guilt. Worse still, five minutes later (while he murdered Scarpio and slopped his penis under the tap), she felt as though nothing whatever had taken place, and that emptiness made hintings of sinfulness take shape in her mind, and the sin seemed greater because of that unfulfilled longing. And when he loped back into the bedroom, still fiddling with his penis like a genital hit-man, she was already out of bed, her nightdress on, tapping a slippered foot impatiently, silently screaming for him to be gone.

In the country, however, it wasn't that simple to summon up a lover for the night. Suddenly Kathleen was shaking with laughter, impossible images scampering aross her mind: herself, naked, heavy breasts flopping, cavorting down the village street, offering her body to the implacable farmers who leaned over their gates and studied her as they might a promising heifer. Still with the trace of amusement on her lips, she fell into an uneasy and fretful sleep.

Before he went to bed, Ignatious Wyett went into every room of his cottage. Methodically he turned certain pictures face to the wall: with every mirror he did the same. In each room he placed an unlit purple candle, and beside each candle a slice of bread, some dried fruit, and a pigeon's wing-feather. He closed and locked every door behind him, putting the keys in a brass box that he kept in the kitchen. Every window was shut tight and bolted, but the curtains he left unpulled. In the kitchen and the bathroom he left the cold water taps trickling. Finally, on the floor of the hallway he laid two bamboo canes, crossed like sabres.

Satisfied, he went upstairs and collapsed, fully dressed, on his bed, his arms stretched wide as though crucified, his palms upwards. Although remaining motionless he seemed to be listening, but there was no sound. Quiet as the grave, he thought. Quiet as the grave wherein my brother lies.

Across the meadows already soaked in dew, the woods were filled with uneasy rustlings. Small animals fretted, scurrying to their kind for reassurance. The bats flew higher than was their norm, and in silence, not, it seemed, seeking nourishment, just flying nervously in wide, unplanned circles. And, while there was no breeze, the leaves stirred restlessly as though trying to break free but transfixed to the trees like moths irrevocably drawn to the mutilating light. And through it all a strange, piercing wail rose into the darkness, a howl as chilling and demented as the woebegone howl of a mutinous wishtonwish.

All night Bridie waited, sometimes dozing, waking with a start, dozing again. But Lady did not come.

· FOUR ·

– YOU'LL NEVER GUESS who's coming to stay with us for the weekend, Mummy said, not looking up from the sink, stroking a pile of bubbles from the washing-up liquid.

It was the last week of August and Bridie was not in the best of humour: the threat of imminent schooling hanging over her hardly fitted in with her scheme of things. Who? she snapped.

– Michael Petty. You remember Michael, don't you? Of course you do, Mummy went on without waiting for an answer. He gave you your watch.

– Oh him. What's he coming here for?

– To visit. He telephoned last night.

– What does he want to visit us for?

– Because he likes us, that's why, Mummy said. Then, noticing the way Bridie was pouting, she added: And you be nice to him, young lady. I want this to be a happy weekend, and I'll have none of your silly tantrums.

– I don't have tantrums.

– Not much you don't, Mummy said, but smiling, admitted her accusations had been something of an exaggeration by adding: Well, not tantrums maybe, but you have a great knack of making people uneasy.

Bridie laughed. I do not, she protested.

– Anyway, let's have fun when Michael comes. Nobody else has bothered to visit us, have they?

– No, Bridie agreed, and appeared content to let the matter rest. But she changed her mind, and asked suddenly: What made him phone you last night? she asked.

– *I* don't know, darling. He just phoned, that's all.

– Oh.

He hadn't, of course. Kathleen Lynch had telephoned him.

– Hello?

– Michael?

– Yes.

– It's Kathleen. Kathleen Lynch.

– Hey. Kathleen. How the devil are you?

– Fine. I'm fine. And you?

– Oh, struggling along as usual. Overworked and underpaid.

– Poor you.

– Yeah. Poor me. So, what's new with you?

– Not a thing. Getting old and haggard.

– I can't see you old and haggard.

– You haven't seen me recently.

– I know.

Kathleen heard the hesitation when she asked: Have you seen Francis?

– No. Well, not to speak to. He was away. I think he's back now.

– Oh.

– Are you all right, Kathleen? You sound – I don't know. A bit strange.

Kathleen gave a tight little laugh. I was always a bit strange, I've been told.

Michael laughed too.

– Listen, Michael, how would you like a few days in the country?

– I'd love it.
– Come down for the weekend, will you?
– This weekend?
– Any weekend.
Michael laughed again, this time with a different timbre. That sounds promising.
– No promises.
– As it happens this weekend would fit in nicely. If I came down Friday evening and left Sunday evening, how would that be?
– Marvellous.
– Okay, then. That's a date.
– Lovely.
– I look forward to it.
– So do I. By the way, Bridie sends her love.
– Oh. Yes. Bridie – how is she?
– Growing up. Quite the young lady now.
– She must be. Not as pretty as her mother though, I bet.
– Far prettier.
– Never.
– Thank you.
– You're welcome.
– I better go. We can talk when you come.
– Will we have time?
– *Plenty* of time, Michael.
– Damn.
They both laughed gaily at that.
– See you Friday evening, then.
– Yep. About eight.
– Lovely.

'So, up until the time you heard that Mr Petty was coming to stay, things had been going well between you and your mother?' the doctor surmises.
'Quite well.'
'Not very well?'
'Quite well,' Bridie repeats.

'Why not very well?'
Bridie shrugs.
'And then Mr Petty came for the weekend?'
'Yes,' Bridie says, her eyes hardening, her mouth clamping on the word.
'Oh dear,' the doctor exclaims. 'That's touched a raw nerve.'
Bridie closes her eyes and does not reply.
'What upset you so about that weekend, Bridie?'
Bridie snaps her eyes open. 'It was horrible.'
'That bad?'
'That bad.'
'In what way?'
'In every possible way.'
'Good gracious.'
Bridie looks away.
'Why don't you tell me about it?'
'What do you want to know?'
'Whatever you want to tell me.'
'I've just told you it was horrible.'
'Yes, but in what way was it horrible?'
'I hated it.'
'I understand that, Bridie. Tell me why, will you?'

Tooting the horn of his new Audi, Michael Petty arrived at the mill just after eight o'clock in the evening. He had dressed, as he thought, for the country: grey slacks, tweed jacket, open-necked Viyella shirt, sensible shoes. He had brought a suitcase which he lifted from the boot, swinging it in a circle before setting it on the ground, putting his hands on his hips, eyeing Kathleen Lynch as she came to meet him. How's the haggard old biddy then?

– Hello, Michael.
– I can see life here agrees with you. You look smashing.
– Thank you.
– Wasted, of course, but smashing just the same.
– Thank you. You look pretty good yourself.
– Clean living, that's my excuse. Like a monk I've been.

Nobody worth lusting after now that you've left us.

– I can just see you as a monk, Michael.

– Cross my heart.

– I believe you.

Michael laughed. Yeah. I can see you do.

Bridie stayed in the doorway, leaning against it, watching, her eyes narrow slits. She saw them kiss each other lightly on the cheek. She saw them stand back, holding fingers, he admiring the old mill, Mummy explaining its quirks and drawbacks. She saw them keep looking at each other, giving shy, coy smiles. She saw Michael Petty touch Mummy's long hair. She saw Mummy run her finger affectionately down the length of his nose. And she was disgusted. Fancy Mummy making a fool of herself like that!

– And this, Mummy said leading Michael by the arm, this is Bridie.

– Well, well, well, Michael said. Goodness you've grown, he added, bending down and already changing his voice to the manner he thought should be used on children. I bet you don't remember me.

– Of course she does, Mummy insisted. Don't you, Bridie? She still wears the watch you gave her. Show Michael, Bridie. Show him the watch he gave you.

Bridie glared at her mother, but she stuck out her arm nonetheless, showing the watch.

– I'm honoured, Michael said. And I've got something else for you in my suitcase. Something for both of you.

– You shouldn't have, Michael, Mummy said, but without much conviction.

– What is it? Bridie asked.

– Bridie! Mummy said. Wait until Michael tells you.

Bridie decided to hate the gift the moment she saw it. Fancy anyone bringing her a stupid doll, made uglier and more loathsome by the way Mummy gushed over it. Isn't that lovely, Bridie? she said, her voice demanding instant agreement.

– Oh lovely, Bridie said sarcastically.

– I didn't realise she'd grown up quite so much.

– It's gorgeous, Michael. If Bridie doesn't want it, I'll have it.

– It's mine, Bridie snapped.

– Well, say thank you, then, and stop being so uppity.

– Thank you, Bridie said, and grabbed the doll, holding it behind her back, trying to gouge out its vacuous eyes with her fingers.

– And this is for you, Michael said, handing Mummy a small, exquisitely wrapped package.

– Oh Michael, Mummy said, giving him a funny look. Whatever can it be?

– Open it, Michael told her.

– It's too pretty to open, Mummy decided, but she opened it anyway, making silly little noises of delight, and gasping when she saw what it was. Look, Bridie. Mummy's favourite perfume. Joy. Oh, Michael. It costs the earth. You really shouldn't have been so extravagant.

– Nothing's too good for you, babe, Michael replied, lilting the words as if purloining them from a pop song.

– You *are* a fool, Mummy told him, getting up from her knees and putting both arms about his neck, pecking him on the cheek.

– As long as it makes you happy.

– You've been far too generous, hasn't he, Bridie? Bridie glowered.

– We both love our presents, don't we, Bridie?

– Oh, we absolutely love them, Bridie said.

'Mummy was so pathetic,' Bridie tells the doctor emphatically. 'You should have seen the way she fell all over him,' she adds. 'It made me sick.'

'Maybe she was just being grateful,' the doctor suggests.

Bridie gives a little dismissive grunt. 'Huh.'

'You must admit it was kind of Mr Petty to bring –'

'He knew what he was doing,' Bridie scoffs.

'What was he doing, Bridie?'

'You can guess what he was doing.'

'I would have thought he just wanted to be kind.'
'Huh. That's not what *he* wanted at all.'
'Oh?'

Michael Petty yawned and stretched himself, and Mummy immediately took the hint. Typical.

– Good heavens! she exclaimed, pretending to be surprised. Is that really the time? Way past *our* bedtime, isn't it, Bridie? she asked, and Bridie, aware of the trickery Mummy was trying to perpetrate, aware, too, that she was being included in the scheme of things in order to make her, hopefully, more amenable, replied: Oh, *way* past our bedtime, Mummy dear. You must be absolutely exhausted.

Stupid, besotted Mummy couldn't even hear she was being sarcastic, and answered: You know, I really am.

– It's all my fault, Michael Petty volunteered.

(Oh, wonderful, brave him, Bridie thought to herself. The gallant knight on the shining steed, no doubt. Huh. Some knight. Pathetic moron, more like, and on a decrepit nag fit for the knacker's yard.)

– Don't be silly, Mummy said. It will do us good to have a change to our routine for once. Anyway, we can sleep in late in the morning.

– Yes, Michael agreed with a quick, mildly lecherous glance at Mummy: a look he immediately switched off when he noticed Bridie watching him intently.

Mummy stood up, and smoothed down her skirt decorously. Your room's all ready, Michael. I'm afraid the bed isn't up to much. I hope you'll sleep all right.

– It'll be fine, I'm sure. I think I could sleep on concrete tonight.

– Well, you won't have to do that, Mummy assured him with one of her twittery little laughs.

– No, Bridie decided to put in. You certainly won't have to do that.

– I've given you the room next to mine, Mummy went on.

– It's ever so handy, Bridie said, and paused, savouring the look of guilt and panic that flashed into Mummy's eyes, before continuing with: for the bathroom.

– Oh. Good, Michael said.

– Yes, Mummy said, letting out her breath.

They were very careful, Michael and Mummy. They waited until they thought Bridie must be well asleep. It was nearly two o'clock before Michael sneaked from his room and pit-patted, barefoot, along the passage. Bridie smiled in cold anger. She heard him open Mummy's door, imagined him slipping into her room, heard him close the door behind him, imagined the excitement on their faces, heard the key turn in the huge, old-fashioned lock.

'It was wicked of her,' Bridie tells the doctor. 'And she only did it to hurt Daddy.'

The doctor looks taken aback by that, and frowns, trying to follow Bridie's logic. 'To hurt your Daddy?' he asks.

'Yes.'

'But your Daddy had left.'

'That's got nothing to do with it,' Bridie snaps angrily.

'I don't follow you, Bridie. What was it your Mummy did anyway?'

'She slept with that Michael Petty. Twice. Friday night and Saturday night.'

'Oh,' the doctor says, nodding as though he could see a glimmer of light. 'And you think your Mummy did that to hurt your Daddy, do you?'

'Of course she did.'

'But your Daddy wouldn't have known.'

'He wouldn't have to know to be hurt. Just because you don't *know* something doesn't mean you're not hurt by it.'

The doctor nods. 'That's true in certain cases. But –'

'There's no buts at all. Mummy deliberately set out to cause Daddy pain.'

'You think your Mummy should have . . .' The doctor stops. The words 'kept herself pure' have filtered into his mind but he finds them archaic, even puerile. He is still fumbling through his vocabulary when Bridie saves him.

'She shouldn't have let herself get dirtied like that,' she says obscurely. 'She knew Daddy would never come back after something like that.'

'And *you* wanted him back badly?'

'*I* didn't *need* him back. He never left me. I told you that already. I wanted him to be back with Mummy. I just wanted all of us together again. Happy, the way we used to be.'

You'd have thought Mummy would have had the wile to check her bed for noise before carrying on in it. But she hadn't, and the springs creaked and twanged, and the headboard banged against the wattle-and-daub wall, rhythmically like an African drum. Bridie heard it all and seethed; when the pleasurable groans and panting began she covered her head with the pillow, pulling the edges down over her ears. How could Mummy be so mean and uncaring? Poor Daddy, out there alone somewhere. Miserable. Wandering about with nobody to love and understand him. Dejected. Maybe crying.

– . . . and they all lived happily ever after, Daddy read, and closed the book gently as though happiness was a fragile thing. Did you like that one, Bridie? he asked.

– Mmmmm. It was lovely. I love the ones that have happy endings.

– That's how it should be. Happy ever after.

– Yes.

– You *are* happy, aren't you, Bridie?

– Oh yes, Daddy.

– And you love your old Daddy?

– Yes. Very much.

– Give him a big hug then.

Bridie sat up in bed and gave old Daddy a big hug, and Daddy hugged her back, holding her very close to him. Then he lowered her gently back on the bed, arranging her hair on the pillow, like a pretty halo, he said. He bent and kissed her gently on the forehead and both cheeks, starting to breathe quite heavily, like he was running although lying down, and, as his mouth, slightly open, moved across her face from cheek to cheek, his lips touched hers, lightly at first in passing, always drawn back to them, pressing down harder each time, his tongue flicking in and out like an adder's, in and out of her mouth, wet and sweet and tasting of the vanilla pudding Mummy had left for their tea before she went out, while his heavy body squirmed its way on top of her, cradling her head in the crook of one arm, his free hand under her pretty blue nightdress, squeezing her tiny, empty breasts, then moving lower, seeking that place Mummy was so fussy about (always making sure it got a special washing in the bath, and was wiped thoroughly with a tissue after every visit to the lavatory), then away again, back to her breasts, breasts that ached now from all the fingering, a strange, pleasurable, inexplicable pain, as something else, something hard and throbbing and alive eased itself between her legs, nestling there for a moment as Daddy gave a sad little moan, then moving again as soon as Daddy moved, moved up and down, up and down like in Ride a Cock Horse, up and down, until suddenly it drew back and plunged down again into her, down, it seemed, right *inside* her, as Daddy covered her mouth with his when she tried to cry away the shooting, searing pain –

– Stop it!

Mummy was in the doorway screaming the words, holding her face in both hands, looking horror-struck.

'Was that when you started to hate your Mummy?' the doctor asks.

Bridie thinks for a moment. 'I suppose it was.'

'Up to that point –'

'No. I hated her before, I think,' Bridie interrupts. 'But I sort of forgave her.'

'What made you hate her before?'

'The way she went on at Daddy all the time.'

The doctor allows himself a tired little smile as though he appreciates the situation. 'Nagging him?'

'She said terrible things to him.'

'Like what, Bridie?'

'I can't remember exactly what,' Bridie lies. 'But I remember they were awful. Daddy used to cry sometimes. It used to frighten me to hear him cry.'

'I'm sure it did,' the doctor says kindly.

'Not that there was anything wrong with Daddy crying,' Bridie adds defensively. 'Just when Mummy *made* him cry it was awful.'

'It would really help me, Bridie, if you could remember some of the things your Mummy said to your Daddy. Anything at all. You must remember something she said that made him cry.'

'I'm sorry, doctor. Honestly I can't,' Bridie insists, shaking her head as though deeply regretting her forgetfulness. 'I really would tell you if I could,' she lies.

– You're nothing but an animal, Mummy continued to scream at Daddy as Bridie, still upstairs in bed, listened. No, Mummy went on, no animal would do to its young what you've done. You're – you're depraved. You're sick. You're –

Daddy tried to say something, his voice muffled, shaking, scared.

– Shut up! Mummy yelled. Don't you dare start trying to excuse yourself this time. I won't stand any more of your damn lies, Francis.

Poor Daddy must have tried again although Bridie heard nothing, but she could imagine him, spreading his hands, his eyes pleading.

– Don't Mummy said, sounding like she was close to tears. Just don't! God, I knew this would happen. I just *knew* it. I'll never forgive you, Francis. As long as I live I'll never forgive you for this terrible guilt you've lumbered me with.

It was early next morning that Daddy went away.

He thought he was ever so clever getting up so early and trying to pretend he had spent the whole night in his own room. But Bridie was waiting for him. Hours before, she had gone to the bathroom and waited. She heard the door of the bedroom open and shut, and she timed it nicely so that she stepped into the passageway just as Michael Petty was half-way between Mummy's room and his own, and at his most unsuspectingly vulnerable.

– Good morning, Mr Petty, Bridie said, using her sing-song, special mocking voice.

Michael Petty jumped. He looked so absurd standing there with only the top part of his pyjamas on, the more so since he immediately shoved his hands forward to cover his dangling penis. Bridie giggled. Are you lost? she asked politely.

– Yes. No. Yes. I thought the bathroom was that way, Michael Petty said, starting to point back down the passage from the way he had come, but immediately slapping his hand over his penis again.

– No, Bridie told him. It's here. I've just been using it.

– Oh. Ah. Thank you, Bridie.

– You're welcome. See you at breakfast.

– Yes.

Old Doctor Foley, nearing the end of his career, a trifle doddery but caring and adamantly refusing to be harassed or bullied by directives, still believing it was his sacred duty to give his patients as much time as they required, never fobbing them off with pills or potions, removed his old-fashioned, steel-rimmed, half-lensed spectacles and took his time about polishing them as though it was not only clarity of vision they enhanced. He found the task confronting him distasteful. The sexual abuse of children appalled him. It was a phenomenon that cropped up with grim, frightening frequency, and he was glad that it would soon be someone else's responsibility to deal with this sad calamity. Carefully he put on his spectacles and leaned back in his leather chair, folding his hands piously. It made it no easier that he had known Kathleen Lynch since her childhood. Well, Kate, he said finally, using the abbreviation that only he had ever used, a familiarity he had first employed when treating her for mumps some thirty years earlier, believing, correctly, that it would ease her anxiety, and using it again now for the same reason.

Well, Kate, I've examined Bridie as you asked, he said. And I'm afraid, as you suspected, penetration did take place.

Kathleen Lynch shut her eyes.

– Fortunately, however, it does not appear to have been a violent assault. There is no vaginal damage.

– Oh, God, Kathleen moaned quietly.

– And there is no fear of pregnancy. However –

Kathleen looked up quickly.

– However, this is a very serious business, Kate. I can understand your reluctance to talk about it, believe me. But, by rights, I should report this to the police, Doctor Foley said, already aware that he would do no such thing, aware that not to do so would be a grave and reprehensible dereliction of duty, but aware, too, that the agony such adherence to medical ethics would bring could far out-measure the pain and bewilderment already being undergone by this unfortunate woman. Besides, he had a shrewd idea who was responsible, and who was he, Septimus Foley, on the point of 'shuffling off this mortal coil', as it struck him, to inflict further suffering, to prolong the tragedy, perhaps to do more damage than had already been done?

– Oh no, Kathleen Lynch pleaded.

Doctor Foley sighed. No, he said kindly. I won't report it, Kate.

– Thank you, doctor.

– If it should happen again –

– It won't. I promise you it won't.

– Can you be certain?

– Yes, Kathleen said vehemently. Quite certain.

– And if it does?

– It *won't*.

Doctor Foley sighed again. Now, as to Bridie –

– You said she was all right, Kathleen said quickly.

– Physically she should suffer no ill effects. Mentally, however, I cannot be sure.

– She seems –

– She seems perfectly fine today, Doctor Foley interrupted. She's very resilient. But if she has suffered any psychological damage it may not show itself for weeks. For months – even years.

– Oh my God, Kathleen almost wailed.

– One thing that may save her – Kate?

– Yes?

– It was Francis, wasn't it?

Kathleen nodded, sobbing now.

– Horrible though that is, it may be a blessing in disguise. The trauma might be less since Bridie clearly loves her father. Only time will tell, of course, but I do think the harm would have been considerably graver had she been assaulted by someone she didn't know.

Kathleen Lynch rummaged in her handbag for a handkerchief. Finding it, she wiped her eyes, giving a weak little smile of apology.

– And that brings us to you, Doctor Foley said sympathetically. Kathleen suddenly pulled herself together. I'm all right, she said. Or I will be in a day or two.

– Oh, I'm sure you'll cope, but –

– You're right, doctor. I'll cope. You're damn right I'll cope, Kathleen answered.

Doctor Foley gave a small, wistful smile. Anger does help, he said. For a while. It's later, when the rage has subsided, that concerns me, Kate. I'd better warn you that in my experience many women, who insist they can cope, soon find themselves visited by a terrible guilt. They blame themselves. It is this guilt that worries me – it is extremely difficult to dismiss. And if it lingers it can cause untold misery.

– Of course I feel guilty, doctor. I should have known it would happen. Dammit, I *did* know it would happen. I just couldn't bring myself to believe Francis would go that far.

Doctor Foley shrugged. That's normal, you know.

– And I'll probably feel guilty for the rest of my life but I certainly won't let it get on top of me.

– I hope not, Kate.

– I won't, don't worry. You can take my word on that.
– Yours is the only word I can take.

Bridie was at her cunning best. She didn't go back to bed but slipped downstairs and started getting things ready for breakfast. She laid the table with considerable care, even transferring a small bowl of flowers from the sitting-room to the centre of the table, and polishing the silver with the chamois Mummy kept in the drawer of the dresser. She used the best china, the cups and saucers and plates with the pretty wild violets painted on them, not the old willow-pattern ones she and Mummy used every day. The packet of cornflakes looked ugly on the table so she filled three bowls and put one ready in each place. She put three slices of bread in the toaster, and three nice big brown eggs in the saucepan of water all ready to be switched on when she heard movement upstairs. She decided on honey instead of marmalade: it smacked more of the country. And she made the butter into little rolls, using the wooden pats expertly. Finally she filled the filter with fresh coffee and turned on the percolator: then she sat down and watched it drip, drip, drip, filling the kitchen with a gorgeous smell.

– Why, how absolutely lovely, darling, Mummy exclaimed, coming to a halt in the doorway, staring in proud amazement at Bridie's handiwork. That *is* kind of you, Bridie. Look, Michael. Look what Bridie has prepared specially for you.

Michael looked, peering over Mummy's shoulder. He looked sheepish and abashed too, which pleased Bridie no end. Lovely, he agreed.

– What a treat, Mummy enthused.
– Sumptuous, Michael said.
– I've never been so spoiled, Mummy went on. You must have been up for hours to get all this so beautifully done.
– Yes, Bridie said. I did get up quite early.

Michael went to work on his cornflakes.

– Something woke me up, Bridie explained. I don't know what it was. Some noise, I suppose.
– Oh dear, Mummy said. What a shame. Still, we wouldn't

have come down to this if you'd slept like I did.

– I'm glad you slept well, Mummy.

– Like a log, Mummy told her.

– Oh good. And you, Mr Petty? How did you sleep?

– I'm sure Michael wouldn't mind if you called him Michael, Mummy put in quickly. Would you Michael?

– No. No, of course not, Michael said, trying to smile brightly.

– Well, Michael, Bridie went on, stressing the name. Did *you* sleep well?

– Very well, thank you, Bridie.

– Oh good.

– And what are we all going to do today? Mummy wanted to know later, getting up and starting to clear the table.

– Here, let me help, Michael volunteered.

– Oh, no, Bridie protested. You're the guest, she said. Mummy and I have to look after you, isn't that right, Mummy?

Mummy laughed happily. Quite right, dear. What would you like to do, Michael?

Michael shrugged. Whatever you want.

Mummy laughed again. Well, to tell the truth, there's not much we *can* do. What do you think, Bridie.

Bridie frowned, then brightened. *I* think, she suggested after a while, that you should take Michael out and show him the village.

– But you'll come with us, won't you?

– I don't think so. Mummy. There's something I want to do.

– Whatever could that be?

– Something.

– A secret?

– Yes. A secret.

– Bridie loves her secrets, Mummy explained to Michael.

– Does she? Michael asked vaguely.

– Oh yes, Bridie said. I have lots of secrets. I know all sorts of things that I keep hidden away.

Michael Petty gave her a quick look.

– I store them up. You never know when they might be useful.

Michael looked at her again, quizzically now.

– She frightens me to death, Michael, Mummy said jokingly. I'm always wondering what she'll come out with next.

Michael Petty didn't seem to think that was all that funny. Oh, he grunted.

– Why don't you and Michael take a picnic, Mummy, and spend the day together. I'm sure you have masses to talk about.

– That's a grand idea, Bridie. Would you like that, Michael?

– Anything that pleases you.

– I'm sure, Bridie said, purposely keeping her voice flat, that whatever pleases you will please Mummy.

– Right, Mummy decided. That's what we'll do. It's going to be a gorgeous day. We could go down to the stream and picnic there.

– Sounds fine, Michael said.

Bridie watched them set off. Michael carried the picnic basket; Mummy carried the rug over her shoulder. They looked very happy together now that they were alone. Like Daddy should have been happy. Happy ever after.

When Ignatious Wyett opened the door he was surprised to see Bridie standing there. Bridie, he said. This is a surprise.

– It's been ages since I called, Bridie said. I've been meaning to. But we've had visitors.

– Visitors, eh?'

– Well, Mummy has a visitor. Someone she knew when we lived in the city.

– Oh. You don't sound too pleased.

Bridie shrugged. He's *her* friend.

– But you don't think much of him?

– Can I come in?

– Of course. I'm sorry. Come in.

Bridie made as if to enter the cottage. She had barely set foot in the hall when she froze. Immediately she recoiled, her face ashen, her eyes wide.

– Whatever is the matter, Bridie? Mr Wyett asked although

not sounding as concerned as might have been expected.

– I don't know, Bridie whispered.

– Did something frighten you?

– No. Yes. I don't know. It felt so cold.

– Cold? But –

– Yes. Freezing. Not like ordinary cold.

Mr Wyett forced a laugh. You're imagining things, child, he said.

– No I'm not, Bridie said, shaking her head.

– Here, Mr Wyett told her, take my hand and we'll go in together.

Bridie backed away. No.

– There's nothing to be afraid of, Mr Wyett assured her.

– No, Bridie said again, twisting her fingers together. I must get home. I must go, Mr Wyett.

– So soon? You've only just arrived.

– I'll come again. Tomorrow. Or the next day.

– Very well. Goodbye, Bridie.

Bridie turned and ran down the narrow garden path without looking back, and Ignatious Wyett went inside and closed the door behind him, leaning back against it, his eyes staring, and filled with sadness and worry. Eventually he heaved himself erect and, as carefully as he had placed them there, he removed the bamboo canes from the floor and stood them upright in the corner by the door. He moved slowly about the house unlocking the windows, and turning the pictures and mirrors right way round. He gathered up the candles one by one and stored them in a grey metal box, and wiped crumbs from the table where the bread and fruit had been. The feathers he burned, watching them curl and disintegrate in the fireplace.

– Bridie saw me leaving your room this morning, you know, Michael Petty told Kathleen Lynch as they sat by the stream.

– She saw you? Kathleen sounded startled.

– Yep. I'm afraid so.

– Oh God. That's all I need.

– You know, if it wasn't ridiculous, I'd say she was waiting to catch me.

– Don't be silly.

– No, I mean it. There was something about her . . . don't ask me what it was . . . a look in her eye . . . the way she spoke . . . something . . . that made me feel she'd been in the lavatory just waiting for me to come out so she could catch me.

– What did she say?

Michael pulled a face. Not much. Asked me if I was lost.

– I don't see that there's much –

– And at breakfast – didn't you notice the snide little undertones she was making?

– No. I didn't.

– I did.

– Now you *are* being silly.

– Maybe. Maybe. There's definitely something odd about her.

– But she likes you, Kathleen protested by way of defending her daughter.

– She *pretends* to like me, you mean.

– Rubbish.

– Can I say something?

Kathleen shrugged. Say anything you like.

– You won't get annoyed?

– That depends, but say whatever it is anyway.

– I also think Bridie only pretends to like you.

Kathleen sat upright, looking shocked and bewildered. Really, Michael. What a preposterous thing to say.

– I know. I know. I know it is. But . . . I can't put my finger on it, dammit . . . but there's a . . . Oh, Jesus, forget it.

– I certainly will. If I didn't know you better I'd say you were off your head.

– Maybe I am. I'm sorry. Here, give me a kiss and make up.

They kissed, not passionately: lovingly like new expectant lovers; like new, expectant lovers who knew their love was doomed. And, as they kissed, Kathleen already felt the impact of Michael's worry clicking in her mind. You're wrong, you know, about Bridie, she whispered in his ear, nibbling the lobe.

– Sure I am. Forget Bridie, will you?

And Kathleen tried to forget Bridie, but later, as they sat in front of the fire Bridie insisted on lighting despite the warmth of the evening, Kathleen watched her daughter and saw a strangeness she had not noticed before. Bridie seemed aloof, withdrawn. She had very little to say for herself and kept casting surreptitious glances in Michael's direction. Once Kathleen caught Bridie staring directly at herself, and when their eyes met Bridie did not flinch: she kept staring and staring, almost as though not seeing, as though she was staring into her very soul, and there *was* a curious glint in her eyes, an inexplicable look that sent shivers up Kathleen's spine.

– Goodbye, Michael. Thank you so much for coming.

– I loved every minute of it.

– I'm sorry Bridie's not here to say goodbye too. I don't know where she is. She goes off by herself.

– Don't let that worry you. You're here.

– Yes. I'm here.

– We must do this again, Michael said, but there was something sorrowful in his tone that implied they never would.

– Yes, we must.

– Bye, then. And take care, Michael said, then frowned suddenly, and looked about him as though expecting to see some unfamiliar sight. Immediately he laughed nervously.

– You're very jumpy, Kathleen pointed out.

– Nerves. The quietness down here is getting to me, I think. Anyway, as I said, you take care.

– I will.

– I'll write.

– Do.

Then he was gone in a flurry of dust as the Audi spun its wheels on the gravel and went rapidly down the lane.

– Is he gone?

Kathleen spun round. Bridie! Where have you been? You might have come and said goodbye to Michael.

– I'm sorry. I meant to.

– Well, you should have made sure to be here. It was very rude of you.

– He didn't exactly come to see me, did he?

Kathleen felt herself starting to blush and turned away. He came to see both of us, she snapped, furious with herself.

– Oh don't be silly, Mummy. I *know* he came to see you. He just wanted to sleep with you.

– Bridie!

Bridie's eyes went into cold little slits. And, of course, you let him.

– That's enough out of you, young lady.

– Was it like sleeping with Daddy?

– I said that's enough.

'I've remembered,' Bridie tells the doctor, smiling brightly as though delighted with herself.

The doctor smiles back. 'Remembered what, Bridie?'

'What you wanted to know the other day.'

The doctor continues to smile as he rummages in his mind, trying to recall what he wanted to know the other day.

'Do you want to know now?'

'Yes. Please.'

'Well, the thing that really made Daddy cry was when Mummy went to bed with that other man.'

'I see,' the doctor says, trying to get his mind back on that track. 'What man was that?'

'That Michael Petty.'

'Who was he?'

'A friend of Mummy's. He came to stay with us in the mill for a weekend. That's when they slept together. I *heard* them sleeping together. And I caught him trying to sneak back to his own room in the morning.'

The doctor looks thoroughly confused but decides to brazen things out. 'I see,' he says again. 'Now let me get this straight, Bridie. This man – Michael Petty – came and stayed for the weekend at the mill?'

'Yes,' Bridie agrees encouragingly.

'And while he was there he slept with your Mummy?'

'That's right.'

'Had he slept with her before?'

Bridie makes a face. 'I don't know.'

'So all you know is that he slept with her at the mill.'

'Yes.'

'But your Daddy was gone by then, wasn't he?'

'Of course he was. Ages before that.'

The doctor clears his throat. 'Then why should your Mummy's sleeping with Mr Petty make him cry? I mean, how would he know?'

'Daddy would know.'

'How?'

'He'd just know.'

'And he'd cry?'

'Of course he'd cry. He'd find it very hurtful.'

The doctor thinks about this for a while, scribbling things down, using more question marks than full stops. Then he looks up. 'Did you talk about this with your mother?'

'About what exactly, doctor?'

'Well, about her making your Daddy cry?'

'No. She wouldn't understand things like that.'

'Wouldn't she?'

'No. She doesn't think that way, you see.'

'Oh.'

'I did let her know I knew she and the man had been sleeping together though,' Bridie tells the doctor.

'And what did she say?'

Bridie giggles. 'She didn't say much. She got really annoyed with me. She's hopeless at keeping secrets.'

'So things were a bit difficult after that weekend? Between you and your mother?'

'Not for me. I knew what I was doing.'

'What about your mother?'

Bridie grimaces. 'She just tried to pretend everything was the same as before.'

'But it wasn't?'
'No. It certainly wasn't.'
'Explain to me.'
'Well, to tell the absolute truth, doctor, it nearly was just like before for a while.'
'What changed that, Bridie?'
'It was after Mr Wyett called to see Mummy.'
The doctor waits.
'He called and they had a long talk.'
The doctor still waits.
'After that things changed.'
'In what way?'
Bridie giggles again. 'I think Mummy was afraid of me.'
'Afraid of you?'
Bridie nods. 'Yes. She even used to lock her bedroom door at night,' she reveals, finding it very funny and bursting out in laughter.
'And you think Mr Wyett's visit had something to do with that?'
'Oh, I'm sure of it.'
'Do you know what they spoke about?'
'No. I wasn't there. But it must have been about me, mustn't it?'
'What makes you think that?'
'Well,' Bridie says, looking very prim, 'I can't for the life of me think what else they'd have in common. Besides, I *think* Mr Wyett knew by then what I was planning with Lady.'
'Mr Wyett knew?' the doctor asks.
'I *think* so.'

– My Wyett! This is a surprise.
– My apologies for barging in on you unannounced, Mrs Lynch, but –
– You're not barging in. I'm just about to make a pot of tea. You'll join me?
Mr Wyett smiled and inclined his head.

– Actually, I've been meaning to invite you over for a meal ever since Bridie told me all about you. Do come in.

– Ah. Bridie.

– Yes, Kathleen said with a tight smile. Bridie. In here.

– To tell the truth, Mrs Lynch, it's about Bridie that I wish to talk to you, Mr Wyett said later. They had been chatting for over an hour, Kathleen speaking rapidly in the manner of someone who has been alone too long, Mr Wyett nodding, agreeing, exclaiming, all the while seeking the moment propitious to introduce the subject of Bridie.

– She hasn't been bothering you, I hope?

– No. No, not in the way *you* mean at least.

– Good. It's difficult for her, you know. She's very grown-up for her age. Sometimes. She's always had the company of adults.

– Yes. She's very grown-up, Mr Wyett agreed.

Kathleen uncrossed her legs and settled herself in her chair, folding her hands on her lap, trying to look alert and interested, waiting for Mr Wyett to say whatever he had come to say. Something about his manner worried her: he was being almost *too* kind, too polite, too – she could not put her finger on it. But it was an attitude she had come across before, she was sure, yet the circumstances of that, too, escaped her for the moment. And behind the extreme kindness and politeness there seemed to be something far less pleasant lurking. It was like, she decided, still patiently waiting for Mr Wyett to speak, like someone giving her an encouraging smile before pulling the carpet from under her.

– Mrs Lynch, Mr Wyett began, I don't want in any way to alarm you but –

– Alarm me? Kathleen asked, immediately alarmed.

– This is so difficult, Mr Wyett said, getting up and staring out of the latticed window towards the woods. So very difficult.

– Whatever can you –

– Mrs Lynch, Ignatious Wyett interrupted, turning from the window, are you a religious woman?

Kathleen looked startled. I – she began.

– I'm sorry to ask. I'm not prying, believe me. I –

– I believe in God, if that's what you mean.

– Ah, Mr Wyett sighed and smiled kindly. People always say they believe in God. I'm afraid it's the other deity I need to know about. The devil. Do you believe in the devil, Mrs Lynch?

– Really, Mr Wyett –

– Please. I need to know.

– Yes. I suppose I believe in the devil. If you believe in God you've – well, you've almost *got* to believe in the devil, don't you.

Mr Wyett nodded, not, however, it seemed, in any agreement with Kathleen's philosophy. And he kept on nodding, encouraging her possibly, when he continued: And as God can fill us with goodness and grace, so the devil can fill us with evil – do you believe that?

Although unable fully to understand why, Kathleen suddenly felt herself consumed with resentment and anger. What has all this got to do with my Bridie? she demanded coldly, her instincts already bristling and spoiling for a fight.

Try as he might, Ignatious Wyett could think of no easy way to say what he believed needed to be said. Recklessly he took the bull by the horns. I am convinced, Mrs Lynch, that little Bridie has been taken over by some tyrannical spirit, he said, almost in a whisper as if this might soften the blow.

For fully a minute, Kathleen sat motionless, literally unable to make herself move, stunned, telling herself (yet at once denying it) that she was the victim of some outrageous, cruel, practical joke. She heard herself give a strained, high-pitched scornful laugh; felt herself start to shake uncontrollably. Tears of fury filled her eyes as she jumped to her feet. I don't know what you think you're up to, Mr Wyett, she spat. How dare you come into my house and start making wild accusations like that? About Bridie! How dare you!

– Mrs Lynch, Ignatious pleaded, reaching out.

– Don't you touch me, Kathleen warned, stepping behind the settee, and don't say another word.

– Mrs Lynch, listen to me. I beg you. Just listen to what I have to say. Then I'll go.

– I don't want to hear another *word*, Kathleen screamed, putting her hands over her ears.

– Please –

– Just go. Get out of my house this instant.

For a moment it looked as though, defeated, Mr Wyett was, indeed, about to go. He walked to the door and opened it. Then, abruptly, he closed it again, and turned, shaking his head. No, he said firmly. I will not go, Mrs Lynch. Not until you've heard me out. I have *got* to try and explain. It's the only hope I have, you see, he confessed mournfully. The only hope I have left to me.

Whether it was the sad, bewildered tone of his voice, or whether it was some instinctive, awful recognition of impending truth, Kathleen Lynch could not at that moment judge, but she felt incapable of further resistance. She sat down again, her eyes fixed on the thin gold wedding-ring she still wore, and turned it round and round on her finger.

Without making a sound, Ignatious Wyett returned to the window, and took to gazing in the direction of the woods again as though culling archaic wisdom and encouragement from the trees. He looked haggard, his cheeks sunken, his eyes swollen, the pupils criss-crossed with tiny scarlet veins giving them the lost aspect of imminent death. The nerve in his finger started to jump, but he ignored it, letting it twitch away. When he finally spoke, his voice was distant and oddly hollow as if transmitted from the periphery of life.

Bridie sat quietly under the owl's great tree, thinking. She was upset. Things seemed to have taken a disturbing turn, and she was confused. The terrible sensation (still inexplicable) she had experienced when attempting to enter Mr Wyett's cottage stayed with her, recurring ferociously at intervals in her mind, frightening her all over again. Yet, perversely, it made her defiant too, as if an heretofore unbeknownst enemy had suddenly declared battle, a mighty, invisible, intangible foe she felt obligated to engage. If only Lady would come and help her! But Lady, it seemed, had other matters on her plate. Her visitations had ceased abruptly since the afternoon she and Bridie had killed Miss Calilly, leaving Bridie out on a limb and feeling abandoned. True, at first she did not worry, putting Lady's absence down to other pressing engagements; but the longer their separation continued the more Bridie contrived to read something sinister into it, always thinking of Lady in human terms, imagining her hurt, or maimed, arrested, even dead.

– They're talking about you, Bridie.

Bridie looked up. There was nobody there that she could see. Everything was still. Very still. No birds flitted between the branches as they normally did in the sunshine, as they had been doing a moment earlier. No animals moved. The trees brooded over her, motionless and solemn.

– Hello, Bridie called. Is someone there?

Her voice echoed away from her: 'lo, 'lo, 'lo, there, there, there. She stood up, listening. Away in the distance a tractor growled. A dog gave a single, sharp bark. Nothing else.

– They're talking about you, Bridie.

Bridie jumped, and swung round. Still nothing stirred. She moved a litle way from the protection of the trees and peered into the mass of trunks and bushes that surrounded her. Nothing. Suddenly she was running, racing, crashing through the undergrowth, oblivious to the savage thorns of the wild blackberry tendrils that ripped at her clothes, running wildly, yet not wanting to run, longing to stop, unable to stop, forced into this headlong stampede as though some demented creature had grabbed her fiercely in tow and was pulling her behind it, dragging her, regardless, out of the woods, intent only on getting her home.

– It is always the innocent who suffer, Ignatious Wyett told Kathleen Lynch. You *must* believe that, he went on, for only then can you appeciate that what I have to tell you is in no way a condemnation of your daughter. She is, I fear, a hapless victim, a child of bright imagination, the perfect prey for the evilness that seeks intelligence and cannot flourish in dullards.

You see evil cannot manipulate the mind that is slow and unreceptive since those minds seem to be endowed with a special protection: it is as though God, admitting to a clumsy blunder, lavishes a unique love on them making their incapacity to shine their greatest safeguard against the corrupter. We all of us have our fantasies, but some, usually those of abundant intellect, cherish those fantasies, seeing them as their own lustrous creation, making of them something real. What starts out as something childlike and charming can, sometimes, through nobody's fault, develop into an outlandish being, a creature of immense potency and wickedness, daemonic and soul-devouring. Bridie, I fear, is possessed by just such a beast.

Mr Wyett fell silent for a moment. He narrowed his eyes and stared intently towards the woods, wrinkling his brow as if suddenly puzzled, his head on one side, straining like someone anxious to hear a faint, enigmatic sound repeated. Then, still frowning and looking perplexed, he turned from the window. Tell me, did Bridie ever mention an owl she saw in the woods? he asked.

Kathleen nodded, not trusting herself to speak.

– And a Silver Lady?

Kathleen nodded again.

– And you thought nothing of it? No, Ignatious continued without waiting for an answer. Why should you? It sounds so pretty, doesn't it? A Silver Lady. We would all dismiss it as the delightful figment any little girl might produce from her mind. Alas, it is anything but delightful. It is an awesome guise sheltering a demon of prodigious power bent on destruction.

Again Mr Wyett paused, turning back to the window, looking out, his eyes darting. All seemed peaceful enough, yet he was convinced he was missing something, overlooking . . . He shook his head, baffled.

– They're talking about you, Bridie.

The words pounded in Bridie's mind as she raced from the woods.

– Hurry, Bridie. Hurry, the voice urged, and Bridie hurried, running as fast as she could down the rutted track, her pretty dress torn at the bodice, a bloody gash down one cheek, her arms stretched out in front of her.

– Hurry, Bridie.

Suddenly Mr Wyett felt himself impelled by an overpowering sense of urgency. He came swiftly across the room and knelt in front of Kathleen. Mrs Lynch, forgive me – please, please forgive me – I must tell you. I am certain that you are in terrible danger. I beg you to let me help you.

– Danger? Kathleen asked vaguely as if just returning from a dream. Danger? she asked again,

– She doesn't want to – I'm sure of that. Probably won't even mean to, but she will kill you, just as she –

– She?

– Bridie.

– Bridie? Kathleen Lynch repeated the name like someone trying to recall someone she had once known, as if the name was familiar but faceless. Then: Bridie? she all but screamed. Immediately she was on her feet, pushing past Ignatious Wyett, almost toppling him. Every protective instinct within her surged to her brain, swamping it. Now I know you're mad, she accused wildly, her arms flapping as if she was trying desperately to release herself from some invisible web of disbelief. I've had enough of your – your – craziness, she said, furious that she could not find the word she wanted. Just get out and stay out. Don't you ever come within a mile of me or Bridie again or I'll call the police. You're – you're *evil*. That's what you are: an evil, wicked old man. Get up off the floor and get out.

Ignatious Wyett buried his head in his arms, muttering to himself.

– Will you get out? Kathleen yelled.

Slowly Mr Wyett got to his feet, unwinding himself, wincing as if every movement was agony. Very well, he said quietly. I will leave you. But promise me you'll be careful.

Kathleen gave him a quick, sharp look, the words sounding strangely familiar. Just go, she snapped.

– Poor little Oliver, Mr Wyett said out of the blue, meaning only to think it.

– What did you say?

– Nothing. Nothing at all.

– You said 'poor little Oliver'.

– Did I? I'm sorry. I –

– Hello, Mummy.

Bridie stood in the doorway, smiling pleasantly at Mummy, ignoring Mr Wyett.

– Bridie, darling, Mummy said, and ran across the room to her, kneeling, holding Bridie close to her. Then she held her at arm's length and studied her. Whatever has happened to you? Look at your face all cut.

– I tripped, Bridie lied.

– You poor angel. And your lovely dress!

– I'm sorry, Mummy.

– It must have been a terrible fall, Mr Wyett said.

– It was, Bridie told him coldly.

– All that damage just by tripping.

– Yes, Bridie said defiantly.

– Mr Wyett is just leaving, Mummy said.

– Oh dear, Bridie sighed with a contented smirk. What a shame.

– You come with Mummy and let her put something on that nasty cut. Goodbye, Mr Wyett.

Bridie hugged Mummy. Yes, goodbye, Mr Wyett, she said over Mummy's shoulder.

'What makes you think Mr Wyett knew?' the doctor asks.

'I'm sure he came to warn Mummy.'

'Oh?'

'But we got there just in time.'

'I see,' the doctor says although clearly he doesn't.

Bridie gives him a nice smile. 'I think, maybe, he *did* warn her. But she didn't believe him of course. We got there before he could convince her.'

'You keep saying *we* got there.'

'Oh, I wasn't alone.'

'No?'

Bridie shakes her head.

'Who was with you?'

'I don't really know,' Bridie tells him, making it transparent that this in no way bothered her.

'Lady, perhaps?'

'No, I don't think so. Someone else. Maybe someone Lady sent while she was busy.'

The doctor nods.

'I didn't *see* anyone, mind.'

The doctor waits.

'I was sitting in the woods and I *heard* someone telling me to hurry home.'

'And, of course, you hurried home.'

'Yes. Yes I did. Very fast. Faster than I've ever run before.'

'And when you got home?'

'Well, once I was there Mr Wyett knew it was pointless trying to say anything nasty about me. I mean, Mummy would always believe me before she'd believe him, wouldn't she?'

'Would she?'

Bridie laughs. 'Of course. Anyway, Mummy sent Mr Wyett home.'

'But his visit had changed her attitude?'

'I think he frightened the life out of her,' Bridie says, laughing again. 'Poor Mummy,' she adds, shaking her head. 'That's when she started locking her bedroom door at night.'

'What else did she do?'

Bridie shrugs. 'Not much else,' she says. Then: 'Oh, yes, she –' Bridie breaks off and rocks with laughter, '– she started wearing a little cross on a gold chain about her neck.'

'And you thought that was funny?'

'Don't you?'

'No. I can't say that I do, Bridie. I think it's very sad.'

Bridie's eyes go cold. 'Oh well,' she says. 'Have it your own way. I thought it was very funny.'

– Good morning, Mummy. You're up early.

Kathleen spun round, startled, forcing a smile on to her tired, drawn face. Good morning, Bridie. I couldn't sleep.

– Oh dear. Is something worrying you?

– No. No. Nothing, Kathleen said quickly.

– Sometimes I can't sleep when something is bothering me.

– There's nothing bothering me, Mummy insisted.

– Good. I thought maybe that silly Mr Wyett had upset you.

– Mr Wyett? No. Why should he have upset me?

– He's weird, that's why. Really creepy, don't you think?

Mummy managed a woebegone smile. He's certainly strange.

– Why did he come anyway?

– Oh, just to chat.

– You both looked so serious.

– Did we? I don't know why.

Bridie gave Mummy one of her funny looks. What did you chat about?

Mummy turned away and straightened the pots of herbs on the window-sill. Nothing much. This and that. The village. The weather. That sort of thing.

– How boring.

– Not really. By the way, there's a card from Michael. He sends his love.

– To me or to you?

– To both of us.

– How nice.

– Bridie, Mummy began later when they had finished breakfast and were clearing the table, you're not – oh, nothing.

– Not what, Bridie pressed.

– Nothing. I'm being silly.

– There *is* something worrying you.

– No, darling. Really there isn't. I was just going to ask – tell me, you are happy here, aren't you?

– Of course, Mummy. Ever so happy.

– You don't mind not having children of your own age to play with?

– Good heavens, no, Bridie exclaimed, using Mummy's favourite exclamation.

– You're not lonely?

– No.

– I just wondered. I thought, maybe, being all alone –

– I've got you, Bridie said sweetly.

Kathleen smiled.

– And Lady, Bridie pointed out.

Kathleen felt every nerve in her body tense.

– And all my little friends in the woods, Bridie concluded.

Kathleen relaxed a little.

– You should come with me sometime, Mummy. All the birds and animals know me now. They're lovely and friendly.

– Yes, Mummy agreed. I must do that, she said before asking, trying to make the question sound casual, and will I get to meet Lady too?

Bridie looked doubtful. I doubt it, she said seriously. Not unless she wants to meet you. She's not very keen on meeting people she doesn't know.

And now, what up until then Kathleen Lynch would have accepted as the childishly charming game of a little girl, seemed to take on a far more sinister aspect, the innocent-sounding words inexplicably filled with foreboding and tragedy, the very admission of Lady's existence threatening her. Ludicrous images swept into her mind, all of them subjugating her motherhood, pointing the finger at her inadequacy, all of them featuring this wretched, menacing Lady as surrogate mother, as foster-mother, indeed as mother, leaving her, Kathleen Lynch, exiled and boycotted, incapable of doing anything but watch her daughter slip away from her.

– Mummy?

Kathleen jumped, and smiled quickly. Yes?

– You're daydreaming.

– Yes. Yes I was.

– I do that sometimes.
– Do you?
– Yes. It's nice, isn't it? You can make up all sorts of things.
– Yes you can.
– And if you think *really* hard, I mean really, really hard you can make anything you like come true.
– I wish that was true, Bridie.
– But it is, Mummy. Honestly it is. I've done it.
Kathleen automatically started to laugh, from habit about to dismiss Bridie's claim as 'play-acting', a term her own mother had a fondness for, using it to cover any childish activity incomprehensible to adults. But she stopped short, her mouth freezing in a grotesque sneer as something Mr Wyett had said reverberated in her brain, something about cherishing fantasies and making them real. She looked directly into Bridie's eyes as she asked: What have you made come true, Bridie?
– Oh just things.
– What things?
– Just things, Bridie said.
Scared, Kathleen found herself getting annoyed. Don't just keep saying *things*. What things?
– Secrets.
Aware that Bridie was digging in her heels and was intent on being stubborn, Kathleen tried another tactic, one that she had employed successfully several times before. She gave a scoffing laugh, and turned away. You are a silly little girl at times, Bridie. Telling stupid stories like that. You really must stop your lies or you'll find yourself in deep trouble one day.
It worked: Bridie flushed scarlet, her eyes dancing with petulance. They're not lies, she hissed.
– Of course they are, Bridie.
– No they're not.
– You can't make things come true just by wishing them.
– Yes you can. *I* can. I've done it.
Kathleen felt her body tense, felt herself quake, too, scared now that she suspected she was about to hear confirmation of Mr Wyett's awful insinuations. Somehow, with a conscious,

rasping effort, she continued her taunting. Of course you have, dear, she said dismissively, tainting her words with sarcasm.

– I have. I have, Bridie insisted, her voice rising shrilly.

– That's what I said: of course you have.

– I have, damn it, Bridie yelled.

The curse startled Kathleen. She had never known Bridie use such language before yet it seemed to come with practised ease. All right, she said turning on her. That's quite enough, Bridie. If you want to be silly, be silly, but don't expect me to go along with it any more. It's high time you grew up.

At first Bridie looked as if she was going to cry, her face puckering. Then, slowly, she backed away from her mother, her eyes assuming that curious blue, glazed, distant effect, her lips working as if she was trying to speak but finding it impossible, tiny flecks of saliva gathering in the corners of her mouth. Suddenly, without warning, she screamed, a high, piercing, demented scream akin to the shrieks of madness, and ran to the door that led into the back garden. She opened it and spun round, shaking with blind fury. You're so clever, she told Kathleen. So very clever.

– You just watch yourself, young lady, or you'll feel the back of my hand, Kathleen snapped more from fear than anger.

– Telling me I'm silly! Well, I wanted Oliver dead, and he's dead, isn't he? Bridie shouted and fled into the garden.

'Almost as funny as her face when I told her I'd killed Oliver,' Bridie says after a lengthy pause during which her attitude has changed, becoming aggressive and bitter.

'You actually told your mother that you had killed your brother?' the doctor asks.

'Not just like that. I simply explained that since I wanted him dead he died. That's all.'

'What did your mother say?'

'Nothing.'

'Nothing?'

'I didn't give her the chance to say anything. I left her standing in the kitchen with her mouth open and went out to play.' Bridie gives a wide smile. 'She was really terrified,' she adds triumphantly.

'And that pleased you, didn't it?'

'Oh yes.'

'And when you came home – what time did you come home?'

'Tea-time about.'

'When you came home at tea-time, didn't your mother say anything about what you had told her?'

Bridie straightens herself in her chair. 'Oh no. Mummy would never have done that,' she says. 'She just pretended our talk had never taken place. She was always scared to talk about things she didn't understand. *That's* why,' Bridie continues, leaning forward now to impress her insight on the doctor, 'she would never talk about Daddy. She didn't understand him at all.'

'But you did? Understand your Daddy, I mean,' the doctor asks, for a moment content to track Bridie's train of thought.

'Oh yes,' Bridie affirms. 'I understood –' she begins before pausing and looking away . . .

– Come and give your Daddy a great big cuddle then, Daddy said, and Bridie raced to him, throwing her arms about his neck, clinging tightly, giving him a great big cuddle, while Mummy watched from her chair, pretending not to be watching, her knitting-needles clicking like a disapproving tongue, the clicks getting sharper and faster the longer Daddy held Bridie in his arms, finally stopping as Mummy put down the little blue and white coat she was making for Oliver and said: It's bed for you, Bridie. You can put the eiderdown over you tonight if you want.

– I want Daddy to tuck me in.

– Your Daddy is probably tired.

– No, he's not. Daddy's never tired. Are you, Daddy?

Mummy gave a sniff. All right. But don't take all night about it. The child needs her sleep. It's way past her bedtime already.

– I was waiting up for you, Daddy, Bridie whispered.

– Comfy? Daddy asked after he had tucked her in.

– Hmmm, Bridie hummed.
– Kiss for Daddy?
Bridie pouted her lips.
Daddy bent down and kissed her.
He kissed her for a long time before he pulled away, looking oddly frightened and very sad. I'm sorry, Bridie, he said.
– What for, Daddy?
Daddy became confused. Nothing, he said. You go to sleep.
– I love you, Daddy, Bridie called after him.
– I love you too, Bridie, Daddy called back . . .
'I understood him very well,' Bridie goes on. 'We were very close, you know.'
'Yes. I can see that,' the doctor says.
'Mummy hated that, of course.'
'Did she?'
'She certainly did. Always snooping about when Daddy wanted to play with me.'
'Maybe she felt –'
'I *know* what she felt,' Bridie interrupts quickly. 'She was jealous, doctor. Now wasn't that silly?'
The doctor grunts, not committing himself.
Bridie stretches herself and makes as if to stifle a yawn. Then she smiles again. 'Anyway,' she says, 'you don't want to hear about all that. What I was trying to tell you was that after I told Mummy about Oliver she never mentioned it again.'

– Mother?
– Oh. Kathleen. This is a surprise. I thought you'd forgotten about me.
– No, mother. I haven't forgotten about you.
– Well, that's something.
– Mother, I need to talk to you.
There was a few moments' silence.
– Mother?
– Yes?
– Did you hear what I said?
– Yes. I'm listening.

– Not on the phone. I want to meet and talk.
– Why can't you tell me on the phone? Kathleen's mother wanted to know, already getting suspicious.
– Because I can't.
– When do you want to come up?
– I want you to come down here.
– Oh, that's quite impossible.
– It's very important, Kathleen pleaded.
– No doubt. But I can't possibly come down to you. Not this week anyway. Nor next. Why don't you come –
– I simply can't, mother. I can't leave Bridie.
– Bring her with you.
– No. I want to talk to you about Bridie.
– Well, it will have to wait, dear.
– It can't wait.
– Then talk to someone else.
– There is nobody else. Not that I can think of anyway.
– What's the matter with Bridie? Mother suddenly asked as if something had just struck her. Is she ill?
– No. Yes. No. She's –
– Really Kathleen you are the limit. Either she is or she isn't.
– Yes she is.
– Well get a doctor.
– It's not that kind of illness.
Her mother clucked with annoyance. What sort is it then?
– She's – she's –
– Can't you go and –
– Never mind, mother. I'll think of something.
Which was easier said than done. Try though she might, Kathleen could think of nothing that would resolve the horror that had engulfed her. In what approached desperation she tried contacting an old Jesuit she once knew only to find he had long since died; however, could the disembodied voice, young and eager, at the end of the telephone line help? Yes, perhaps he could. He would try: he was listening. Poor Kathleen stuttered and stumbled through the litany of events, divulging Mr Wyett's sinister explanations, revealing her own emotional

turmoil and, in the end, waiting for consolation, but left wondering how silence humming down the telephonic lines could possibly be so accusing, could transmit the Jesuit's incredulous, smirking face, could make her feel like a moronic neurotic, could leave her feeling more isolated and desperate than before, leaving her shaking and trembling as if Ignatious Wyett's evil spirits had invaded the telephone line and were gleefully distorting everything she said so that it was heard at the other end as the insane babbling of an hysterical woman seeking dramatic attention. Then, her confusion and loneliness and frustration increasing (and the more addled and isolated and alienated she became, the more imperative it seemed that she speak to someone understanding), she telephoned Michael Petty. At least he was sure to be sympathetic, was he not? No, alas, he was not. He was far too busy. He was inundated with work. Clients were, he claimed, queuing up to see him and he had no idea how he was going to cope. Could she call him back in a day or two? Better still, could she wait until he had time to call her back and give her his undivided attention? God, he was sorry. He truly was very sorry he couldn't listen. She had no idea how hectic things were right now. Francis? That surprised him. But no, no, he had no idea where Francis could be found. Hadn't he gone back to Egypt? No, well, he still didn't know where he was. But yes, definitely, he would try and find out and, the moment he did, he would phone her back. Oh, get Francis to phone her? Yes, sure, of course, he would do that. Meanwhile she was to stop being silly. No, of course he didn't think she was trying to abuse his friendship. Indeed, he really appreciated her call, was flattered that she had come to him, he was just sorry he couldn't give her his full attention at the moment. Yes, he promised, he would do his best to locate Francis and tell him to be sure and phone. Yes, immediately and without delay. But he really did have to hang up now.

Of course Francis didn't call, not within three days anyway, and by that time Kathleen Lynch was at the end of her tether. True, thankfully, there had been no more incidents. Bridie had been distantly polite, and Kathleen had been grateful for that, carefully preserving the uneasy truce, not mentioning Bridie's claim to have somehow wished into existence Oliver's death, not discussing anything much in fact, keeping silent as much as possible, limiting her conversation to everyday banalities, maintaining a calculated outward calm, believing, for some reason, that any sign of her weakening would be calamitous. It was only when she discovered the doll that she realised she could no longer pretend everything would clear itself up like measles.

The discovery was quite fortuitous. As a matter of principle Kathleen never rummaged in Bridie's cupboards, remembering how she had loathed her own mother searching hers, demanding: what's this, what's that for, where did you get this, why do you want to keep that? It just so happened (almost as an inexplicable act of reconciliation) that Kathleen decided to tidy Bridie's room for her. That done, she happened to glance out of the window and spotted dark clouds, presaging rain, looming up from behind the hills. That brought thoughts of winter to her mind, and it struck her it might be a good idea to air the winter blankets. She opened Bridie's cupboard and pulled down two woolly blankets from the top shelf. Something fell at her feet.

The blankets still tucked awkwardly under her arm, Kathleen knelt down, and stared, disbelieving, at the mutilated doll on the floor. She dropped the blankets and picked it up, feeling herself go suddenly cold. The eyes were gone, gouged out savagely, the stuffing oozing from the gaping holes like dried pus. Both hands and both feet had been severed. Its hair had been ripped out, its clothes removed. The material between its legs had been torn apart and the shaft of a screwdriver inserted. Through its heart a hat-pin had been driven. Round its neck a small, brown identification tag had been tied, and on this was written 'Mummy'.

Remarkably Kathleen felt no inclination to panic. She was very cool and collected as she stood up and returned the doll and the blankets to the cupboard, replacing them exactly as they had been, closing the door, even giving the handle a little rub with the hem of her apron.

Ignatious Wyett lay in bed, wondering what had woken him. Then he heard the knocking on the door. Bewildered and sleepy, muttering to himself, he slipped on his overcoat and went downstairs, glancing at the grandfather clock: three o'clock in the morning was not, by any standards, the time he would choose to entertain. He switched on the light and opened the front door.

– Mrs Lynch!

– I'm sorry to come at –

– Don't apologise. Do come in. Come in.

– I had to talk to you, Kathleen said, sitting. Nobody else would listen, she added bitterly.

– No, Ignatious said. People don't like to listen.

– I wouldn't have bothered you only –

– You're not bothering me. I prayed you would come.

– I think you were right about Bridie, Kathleen admitted, hating herself, feeling the guilt of betrayal.

– I'm sure I was. And I understand how difficult it must be for you to come and tell me that.

– Yes.

– But something more has happened?

Kathleen nodded. Yes.

Ignatious Wyett sensed that Kathleen wanted time to reveal why she had come, so he poured brandy into two tumblers, and sipped his as he offered her the other.

– Oh. Thank you . . . Mr Wyett, I found something today, something that . . . Suddenly Kathleen started to shake, tears streaming down her face, and Ignatious turned away, going to his chair, easing himself into it, avoiding looking at the sobbing woman, aware that he could, as yet, do little to comfort her.

– I'm so sorry, Kathleen soon apologised, sniffing, trying a little smile.

Mr Wyett nodded sympathetically and smiled back.

Kathleen drank some brandy and straightened her

shoulders. I was taking some blankets out of Bridie's cupboard this morning – I wanted to air them – and I came across a doll a friend of mine had given her only a couple of weeks ago. It was horribly mutilated. Horrible, Kathleen repeated, shuddering. Its eyes had been poked out. No hands. No feet. The handle of an old screwdriver had been pushed into . . . Kathleen stopped, shaking her head. Had been pushed between her legs, she went on. There was a hat-pin in her heart. And – well, there was a tag round her neck with 'Mummy' written on it.

Ignatious nodded, quite calmly under the circumstances. Yes, he said. That would fit.

– Fit?

Ignatious sighed. Yes, I'm afraid so.

– You mean Bridie wants – intends – to –

– No. Not Bridie. Someone inside Bridie. That's what I was trying to explain to you the other day –

– When you said I was in danger?

– Yes. Can you get me that doll?

– Yes. Of course.

– Good. As long as we have that doll you should be safe.

– What on earth has the doll got to –

– Images, Mrs Lynch. Images. That's what we are dealing with. We have so little time, though. Where's Bridie now?

– At home. Asleep.

– The doll is in her room?

– Yes.

– In the morning then. As early as you can get to it without Bridie knowing, I want you to bring me that doll. Don't meddle with it. I must see it exactly as it is.

Kathleen nodded. Bridie usually goes out about half nine. I can get it then.

– Good. She doesn't know you're here?

– Oh no. She was fast asleep when I came out. I looked in to make sure.

– Good, Mr Wyett said again. I'll see you later today. Meanwhile I have many things to do. You go home and get some rest. And don't worry. Leave everything to me.

Bridie heard Mummy open the door of her bedroom and peep in, checking to make sure she was asleep. Bridie had been asleep but had been awoken by someone whispering to her. Bridie, the voice said, wake up, my darling. So Bridie woke up, instantly alert. She heard the springs on Mummy's bed creaking.

– Your Mummy's getting up.

– I can hear that.

– She's getting dressed.

– Is she?

– I think she's going out.

– At this time?

– Where is she going, Bridie?

– I've no idea.

Mummy opened the door and peeped in to make certain Bridie was asleep, and Bridie pretended to be, keeping her eyes shut and breathing gently, smiling inwardly at Mummy's stupidity.

– Do you think it will rain today, Mummy? Bridie asked pleasantly.

– Oh I don't think so.

– Oh good. Can I stay out until tea-time?

– If you want, Bridie.

– I thought I'd take some chocolate with me and spend the day alone, thinking.

– Thinking? All day? About what?

– Oh, lots of things.

– If that's what you want.

– Thank you, Mummy, Bridie said politely and left the kitchen by the back door, setting off for the village to get her chocolate.

Once Bridie was out of sight Kathleen hurried upstairs, making straight for the cupboard. She started to panic when she could not find the doll. She pulled everything out, throwing blankets and sheets, clothes, shoes, everything on the floor, but there was no doll. She collapsed on the pile of blankets, hugging herself, weeping, moaning inconsolably.

She was still there at midday, huddled and scared, when the telephone rang downstairs. Kathleen rushed down to answer it.

– How are you Kathleen?

– Francis! Oh, Francis. Thank you for phoning.

– Mike. Mike Petty told me you needed to talk to me.

– Oh God, Francis, I do.

– You sound – Francis gave a small disbelieving laugh – frightened.

– Francis I'm terrified. Can you come down – please?

– If you want me to, of course I'll come down.

– Oh, thank God.

– I'll be there this evening.

– Thank you, Francis. Thank you. Thank you. Thank you.

– Gone? Ignatious Wyett sounded appalled.

– I'm afraid so. I've hunted everywhere and there's no sign of it.

– Oh my God, Mr Wyett moaned.

– It doesn't matter now, Mr Wyett. Francis is coming down. He'll soon –

– Doesn't matter? Of course it matters. It matters desperately. It's the crux of – who's Francis?

– My husband.

– Husband? I didn't think you –

– We're separated.

– You've told him about Bridie?

– No. Not yet. I will when he gets here.

– No. Don't do that, Mrs Lynch. Don't tell him anything yet. Let me speak to him first. Please.

– Why on earth –

– Just trust me. Let me speak to him before he knows anything.

– But he's only coming because I said I was terrified.

– I'm sure that's not the only reason. Can you fob him off until we've spoken?

– I don't know. I can try I suppose.

– Please do that, Mrs Lynch. Try as hard as you can.

– All right.

– Does Bridie know her father is coming?

– No. I haven't seen her all day.

– Ah. Good.

– But she'll be home before he arrives.

– Let's hope that doesn't matter.

Kathleen was forced into a little laugh. You're being so –

– I wish I could laugh too, Mrs Lynch.

– I wasn't laughing at –

– I know. Forgive me. Just please remember it is imperative I speak to your husband as soon as possible.

– I'll remember. Don't worry. I'll have him contact you this evening.

– Thank you. Now, about that doll . . .

– Oh, Kathleen said, feeling herself go tense again. Yes. That doll.

– There is no need to look for it any more. You won't find it now.

– Maybe it's –

– You won't find it, Mrs Lynch, Mr Wyett said firmly. Just be extra careful from now on. Please.

– I will. Francis will look after me anyway.

– I hope he can. I certainly hope he can.

'And then, of course, Daddy came to stay,' Bridie tells the doctor.

'*That* must have pleased you.'

'It should have,' Bridie concedes.

'Didn't it?'

'At first, yes. At first I was very pleased to see him.'

(Daddy, Daddy, Daddy, Bridie cried in delight when she looked out of the window and saw him getting out of his car. Mummy, it's Daddy, she called and ran out to meet him, her arms thrown wide, expectant of one of his great big hugs. But Daddy was different. Hello, Bridie, he said, fondly enough, but he didn't return her embrace with much enthusiasm, and he kept looking at Mummy as she came slowly from the house, standing up when she drew near and easing Bridie to one side, putting his arms around Mummy instead, kissing her on the cheek, and saying 'I've missed you' in a soft, tender voice, staring into her eyes.)

'Only at first?' the doctor asks.

Bridie nods.

'And what happened to change your mind?'

'Nothing *happened*. It was Daddy. He was different.'

'In what way was he different, Bridie?'

'Just different.'

(He barely looked at her, his eyes following Mummy's every move, being very polite and careful, saying what a pretty place the mill was and how wonderfully Mummy had decorated it, saying he'd often wondered what it was like, saying it wasn't a bit like what he'd imagined, but didn't Mummy get lonely so far away from the city, how ever did she pass her time; and Mummy tittering coyly and explaining that she didn't have half enough time to do all the things she wanted to do, and saying how well he looked, and hadn't he lost weight, and how whatever he was doing must be agreeing with him, and oohing with praise when he told her he'd stopped drinking, but still, alas, smoked too much, and Mummy forgiving him instantly, replying that he couldn't give up all his bad habits overnight, could he, and it was great that he had stopped drinking, really brave since it must have been difficult, protesting that it simply couldn't have been as easy as Daddy said it had been, and golly – golly! – they had so much to talk about, to which Daddy agreed, saying that they would have to have a session later when they were alone, glancing at Bridie as if she was in the way.)

'That doesn't tell me much, Bridie,' the doctor points out. 'Did he *look* different?'

Bridie shakes her head. 'No. Not really. A bit thinner, maybe.'

'So it was his attitude that had changed?'

'Yes.'

'Towards you?'

Bridie nods, and for a moment looks close to tears.

The doctor decides to wait.

Bridie sniffs away her sadness. 'It was Mummy's fault, of course,' she says. 'Every time he went to talk to me she would interrupt him with some stupid question. I could see he wanted to take me on his knee and cuddle me, but Mummy was determined not to let him.'

The doctor listens without interrupting.

'Even when I said I was going to bed and Daddy asked could he tuck me in like old times, Mummy stopped him. She said I was far too old for that now.'

(Bridie got to her feet. I'm going to bed now, she announced.

– Oh. Good night, then, Bridie, Mummy said, barely looking up.

– Will you tuck me in, Daddy?

Daddy laughed. Oh, you're far too big for that sort of thing now, Bridie, he said. Only little girls get tucked up by their Daddy. You're quite the young lady now, aren't you?

– I want you to tuck me in, Bridie said, trying hard not to show her annoyance.

– Don't annoy Daddy, Mummy said, giving Daddy a small, grateful smile.

Bridie threw her a furious look.

Daddy saw it. You go on up to bed, he told her. Maybe I'll look in later with Mummy. We'll both tuck you in.

– I want *you* to tuck me in.

Daddy tried to dismiss her with another laugh. I'm out of practice with tucking little girls into bed, he said, looking away, looking at Mummy again. Besides, I'm so tired I don't think I'd manage all those twisty stairs.

– Don't be such a nuisance, Bridie, Mummy put in. Can't you see Daddy wants to rest? We'll both come up later and say good-night.

Bridie seethed with anger and bitterness, but she decided to try a different tactic. No, she said. Don't do that. You'll only wake me up. I'm just being silly.

Mummy and Daddy exchanged looks.

– Good night, Mummy, Bridie said, moving to Mummy and offering her cheek for a kiss.

Kathleen kissed her lightly. Good night, dear.

– Good night, Daddy, Bridie said, preparing to put her arms about Daddy's neck and love him.

– Good night, Bridie, Daddy said, grasping her arms and holding her away from him, only giving her the smallest peck on her forehead.)

'That must have made you angry,' the doctor suggests.

Bridie shrugs. 'Not really. I just didn't care. I knew it wasn't Daddy's fault. He'd have tucked me in if Mummy had let him.'

'Still –' the doctor hints.

'Still nothing,' Bridie snaps. 'Anyway, *I* was tired too. So I went to bed and fell asleep immediately.'

(Bridie went sullenly to her bedroom, taking her time going up the creaky stairs, muttering darkly to herself. She could hear Mummy and Daddy talking downstairs, talking earnestly, but in quiet, friendly tones. She shut the door of her room behind her and leaned against it. Then, on tiptoe, she walked to the corner nearest the window and bent down. She took the yellow, flower-shaped clip from her hair and used it to ease up a section of the floorboard. It came up easily. Smiling, Bridie pulled out the doll. She placed it on the floor and knelt beside it. She withdrew the hat-pin, feeling its point gingerly with her finger. Then, her face suddenly contorting, her eyes alight with demented fury, she started stabbing the doll, plunging the hat-pin into its heart over and over, stopping only when overcome with exhaustion.)

'But you must have been very angry with your mother?' the doctor insists.

'I didn't have to be,' Bridie tells him with a knowing smile. 'I knew I could deal with her any time I wanted.'

– Mr Wyett? Francis Lynch. Kathleen, my wife – she said you wanted to see me urgently.

And from that moment on, Francis Lynch wondered what he had let himself in for, wondered if he found himself in the presence of a raving madman, wondered if he had been little more than a damn idiot for believing everything Kathleen had told him. Now, sitting in Mr Wyett's cottage, drink in hand, a generous drink admittedly, Francis Lynch, who had made the journey from the city accompanied by nervous curiosity and, more importantly, by the hope, faint but nevertheless existent, that a reunion with Kathleen was on the cards, whose life had been a tangled pattern of despair and remorse but who had made a conscious, determined effort to overcome the perverse nightmare that stalked and taunted him, who *had* overcome the perverse nightmare that had stalked and taunted him, who believed his luck had changed, who longed genuinely for nothing more than one final chance to prove he was not the monster he might well once have been, who had reconciled God insofar as he could go to Mass again without feeling Christ's baleful eye staring him between the shoulder-blades, listened in annoyed astonishment (and, admittedly, with something akin to amusement as well) as Ignatious Wyett, looking wild and half-mad, launched himself into what Francis could only think of as a diatribe of outlandish proportions against some daemonic evil he was convinced had invaded Bridie's mind, but not before he had managed to demand: What is all this nonsense you have been telling Kathleen?

– Ah. She told you.

– Of course she told me.

– And you believe it is nonsense?

– Yes. Total nonsense.

– I was afraid you might, Mr Wyett acknowledged, and then he was off, pacing the room, throwing his arms about, ranting, as Francis saw it, about evil's stealthy bailiff surreptitiously infiltrating Bridie's soul, about straddling the gaping chasm that divided knowledge and faith, about shunting echoes of hope and mercy that weaved dreadful visions of what *is* and concealed what *seemed* to be, yet all the while, it struck Francis (no matter how fatuous or haphazard or bleak his sermon appeared on the surface) forging towards a definite, predetermined, precise climax. On and on the words tumbled, buffeting Francis's mind until, at length, their tumult and incomprehensibility made him switch off, leaving them to rattle about the room like dried peas on a drum.

Bridie was out of bed in a flash. She scuttled to the window and stared out at Daddy walking down the short drive, standing back a bit so he wouldn't see her if he happened to glance up.

– What's he up to, Bridie?

– I don't know.

– It's very strange him going out at this time.

– Very.

– He doesn't even know anyone in the village, does he?

– No. I don't think so.

– He can't just be going for a walk.

– No.

– Maybe Mummy has sent him somewhere?

– Maybe.

– But where?

– I don't know.

– She's so devious, you never can tell what she's up to.

– Poor Daddy.

– I wouldn't waste sympathy on him now, Bridie. He hasn't been very nice to you.

– He will when we're alone.

– You think so?

– I'm sure.

Bridie saw Daddy turn towards the village.

– He's going to see that Mr Wyett, Bridie.

– I thought that.

– Mummy definitely put him up to that.

– Yes. I know.

– She's trying to turn him against you. That's what she's doing. You know that, don't you?

Bridie smiled coldly. She can try.

The voice in her head cackled. Yes. She can try. But we won't let that happen.

– No.

– We can make sure she never interferes again, can't we?

– Yes. Oh yes. We can make sure of that all right.

Bridie moved quickly now, doing everything methodically as though she had long since rehearsed the procedure. She put on her dressing-gown and slippers. She combed her hair and primped herself in front of the mirror. She took the doll from under the floorboards again and removed the hat-pin from its heart, secreting it up her sleeve, weaving it twice through the material so that it would stay there safely. She went along the passage to the bathroom and ceremoniously washed her hands; then she went downstairs without making a sound.

Mummy was in the sitting-room, reading, or pretending to read, flicking through the pages of a magazine that claimed it knew how she could get the most enjoyment from her garden. (Use your imagination to the full and don't be limited by the boundaries. Aim for a riot of colour throughout the year.) She was seated on the low, red and gold leather pouffe that someone had brought back from Suez, leaning forward, the magazine on her lap, her back to the door, her head bent. Bridie smiled from the doorway.

The silence was so abrupt and unexpected that Francis reacted as if startled by a loud noise.

– Ssh, Mr Wyett warned, holding up one hand, cocking his head to one side.

Francis, too, listened but could hear nothing untoward. It struck him that this respite was a godsend in which he could make his escape, and stood up.

– Your wife is at home? Ignatious demanded.

– Yes.

– With Bridie?

– Yes.

– Dear God, Mr Wyett whispered, clearly distressed. We must hurry, he added, leaving the room at the trot.

– Mr Wyett –
– Come *on*, Ignatious urged. Hurry.

Bridie eased the hat-pin from her sleeve, grasping the ornamental decoration tightly. She picked her way across the room, her slippers silent on the floor, holding her breath, matching each pace to each page Mummy turned.

'So it was about that time you decided to kill your Mummy, was it?'

Bridie frowns. 'I think so,' she admits willingly.

'Without the help of your Lady?'

Bridie's eyes brightened. 'You know, that hadn't struck me before,' she says, delighted by some realisation. '*That's* why it didn't happen the first time. Of course, doctor. That's why.'

'You mean you tried to kill your mother once and failed?'

'Yes. But, you see, I hadn't got permission from Lady so she stopped me.'

'How did she do that, Bridie?'

'She made Daddy and Mr Wyett arrive before I could do anything.'

Bridie eased her way forward, the hat-pin already slightly raised, her eyes staring. Then she stopped dead.

– Back to bed, Bridie. Quickly. Back to bed.

With uncanny speed Bridie turned and fled silently from the room, racing up the stairs two at a time. She had just reached her bedroom when she heard the kitchen door crash open and Daddy's voice calling: Kathleen? Kathleen? Kathleen? anxiously.

– In here, Francis, Mummy answered. Whatever is the matter?

Then Mr Wyett asked: Where's Bridie?

– In bed.

– You're sure?

Mummy didn't answer that, maybe she didn't have time to answer since immediately Bridie heard people running up the stairs. She leapt into bed and pulled the blankets up to her chin, closing her eyes. Her door opened.

– There. You see, Mummy said in a whisper. I told you. Sound asleep.

– Thank God, Mr Wyett said.

They closed the bedroom door quietly and went downstairs, talking but keeping their voices low. Giggling to herself, Bridie got out of bed and opened her door. She squatted on her haunches, listening.

– Of course she didn't, Mummy said. I've been sitting here reading a magazine – that magazine.

Mr Wyett didn't seem able to believe that. And she never came near you?

– No. I've been here in this room by myself since Francis went to see you.

Bridie smiled contentedly and imagined Mr Wyett shaking his silly head.

Mr Wyett shook his head. I *know* she was in the room with you.

– I tell you she wasn't, Mummy insisted.

Daddy coughed. Look, he said, I –

– I know. I know, Mr Wyett interrupted. You think I'm mad, he said disconsolately.

– Since you put it like that: yes, Daddy agreed.

– It must, indeed, seem that way, Mr Wyett allowed. This is the craftiness of it all. Discredit me and –

– Of *what* all? Daddy demanded, sounding quite vexed now, like he wasn't about to put up with much more.

Mr Wyett started explaining, talking rapidly but in little more than a whisper. Bridie strained to hear. She crept to the top of the stairs and sat down: still the words were just a jumble. She moved down the stairs on her bottom, shutting her eyes as if this might help to make the words clearer. Suddenly the sitting-room door was flung open:

– Ah, Bridie, she heard Mr Wyett say distinctly.

Bridie opened her eyes in alarm and saw Mummy and Daddy and that horrible Mr Wyett all standing in a group at the foot of the stairs looking up at her questioningly.

– What are you doing there, Bridie? Mummy wanted to know.

Bridie recovered her composure quickly. She stood up and yawned and stretched and summoned up a lovely big smile, beaming it exclusively at Daddy. I think your talking must have woken me up, and I felt ever so thirsty, she explained. I was just coming down to get some milk.

Mummy looked at Daddy and Daddy looked at Mr Wyett. Mr Wyett kept his eyes fixed on Bridie's face. You were sitting on the stairs, he said.

– Yes, Bridie agreed with a merry little titter. I nearly fell down. I tripped on my dressing-gown, you see.

Mummy gave an exasperated sigh. Well, go to bed and I'll bring you up a glass of milk.

– Can Daddy bring it?

– No. I'll bring it, Mummy said.

– All right, Bridie replied. Thank you, Mummy.

– And you thought he was your friend!

– Yes.

– But you see now that he has turned against you, don't you?

– Yes.

– He's your mother's friend now.

– Yes.

– She's taken him away from you too.

– Yes.

Alone, snuggled down in bed, the thoughts whirred in Bridie's head. How could Mr Wyett be so unkind? Oh, well, she was alone now. Except for Lady. And she was the only friend she *really* wanted.

– I'm your only friend now, Bridie.

– I know.

– Even your Daddy –

– I don't want to talk about Daddy.

– No. No, of course not. I understand.

– Do you? Really?

– Of course I do.

'And you really think it was your Silver Lady who prevented you the first time?' the doctor asks.

'Oh absolutely. That time wasn't right, you see. Everything has a right time, doctor. That's why she told me to go back to bed and sent Daddy home so quickly.'

'Oh *she* told you to go back to bed?'

'Of course. That's obvious.'

The doctor smiles and waggles his head. 'Not so obvious to the rest of us, Bridie.'

Bridie smiles back encouragingly.

'And what do you think might have happened if you hadn't obeyed Lady's warning and gone back to bed?'

'I'd have been caught, wouldn't I?'

'So you think Lady actually prevented you from getting caught?'

'Of course.' Bridie sounds surprised.

The doctor nods. 'But you were caught in the end.'

'Ah yes,' Bridie agrees, smiling indulgently. 'But it was the right time for me to be caught.'

'Ohhhhh.'

'*That's* the difference, you see.'

– I just don't know what to believe, Kathleen whispered to Francis.

They were lying together in bed, and were there by tacit, mutual agreement. The fact that they were about to sleep together had been neither discouraged nor disputed. After they had seen Mr Wyett out of the door they had simply gone upstairs, their arms about each other's waist, and made their way to Kathleen's bedroom, stripped, washed, brushed their teeth, and got into bed almost as if there had never been a break in their union.

– I honestly don't know what to believe, Kathleen whispered again, nestling her cheek comfortably on Francis's shoulder, feeling secure with his arm about her.

Francis gave a low chuckle. Well, I can tell you one thing. I don't believe that lunatic Wyett, and that's for sure. He's nutty as a goddam fruit-cake.

– I don't know, Francis. He was right when he signalled to us that he felt Bridie was listening on the stairs.

– Huh. Chance. Pure chance. Or he simply heard the stairs creak.

– And another thing. You know when he seemed so surprised when I told him I'd been alone in the sitting-room until you both came crashing in?

– Yeah.

– And how he seemed positive Bridie had been in the room with me?

– Mmmm.

– Well, just before you arrived I could have sworn there *was* someone in that room with me. I even looked round.

– But there was no one?

– No. No one.

– Well then. Stop worrying.

Kathleen snuggled closer, purring as Francis ran a finger up and down her spine. She wrinkled her nose as his familiar body odour filled her nostrils, filled her mind, too, with tiny, suddenly recalled, happy fragmented episodes in their marriage that she had excluded from her memory, shoving them brutally into the unused attic of her mind.

– Comfy? Francis asked.

– Yes. Very. Francis? What about the doll?

– What about it?

– Well, it wasn't very nice, was it? Finding it mutilated and stabbed with my name on a tag round its neck.

– You know what Bridie's like. She can be bloody bad-tempered at times. You probably did something to annoy her so she decided to take it out on the doll.

– You think so?

– I'm sure so. Stop worrying and get some sleep. We'll work something out tomorrow.

– Yes. Thanks.

– You're welcome.

Bridie heard Mummy's bed creak as Mummy and Daddy got into it and she had a hard time holding back the tears of anger that forced themselves into her eyes. She was even, for a brief moment, angry with Lady for stopping her: had she been allowed to kill Mummy she wouldn't be there in bed with Daddy now. Bridie would have him to herself. Not sharing her with horrible Mummy who slept with other men.

– There's no need to be angry, Bridie. You'll have Daddy all to yourself soon.

– Will I?

– Of course you will. I promise. You must never rush into things though, or you'll find yourself in all sorts of trouble.

– Yes. I'm sorry.

– You won't have to wait too much longer.

– How much longer?

– Soon. Very soon.

– Promise?

– I promise.

And with that promise Bridie fell asleep, feeling soothed, feeling warm at the prospect of having Daddy all to herself soon.

'Do you mind if I ask someone else to sit in on our next few sessions?' the doctor, the nice doctor who looks a bit tired these last few days but who still keeps his neat row of pens and pencils in the top pocket of his white coat and writes down almost everything Bridie says on his pad and who nearly always speaks in a soft, coaxing voice although a few times making it sound sharp when Bridie surprises or outwits him, asks.

Bridie is not at all sure about that. 'Who?'

'A colleague. A friend.'

'Why?'

'Why would I like him here? Oh, no particular reason. I just want him to listen and perhaps give me his opinion when we've finished. I value his opinion.'

'Is he important?'

'Not important, I wouldn't say. But he's very clever.'
'Cleverer than you?'
The doctor laughs pleasantly. 'Much cleverer than me.'
'Is he nice?'
'Very nice. I'm sure you'll like him.'
Bridie frowns her uncertainty. 'I don't know,' she says.
'Think about it. Maybe you'll change your mind.'
'Maybe I will,' Bridie agrees. 'But probably I won't.'
But she does. She changes it that afternoon and says: 'That will be quite all right, doctor. You may have your friend in to listen.'
'Thank you, Bridie. I appreciate that.'
So the doctor's colleague and friend comes into the room and shakes hands with Bridie, and says, smiling just the way Daddy smiles: 'I'm very pleased to meet you, Bridie. I've heard a lot about you. I'm Paul Maddox. I hear you're a very bright young lady.'
Bridie glows in the compliments, and manages to blush nicely. 'I'm pleased to meet you too, Paul Maddox,' she says with a disarming smile, and they both laugh at the way she has used his name.
'You see, Bridie? I told you he was very nice.'
'Yes,' says Bridie.
'Shall we make a start?'
'If you want. If Paul Maddox is ready to listen so he can give his clever opinion later.'
'I think you know what I want to talk about today,' the doctor says.
Bridie grins. 'Yes. I think I do.'
The doctor waits.
Paul Maddox waits too.
'You want to talk about when I killed Mummy, don't you?'
The doctor nods. 'Yes. Yes I do. You see, Paul, I told you Bridie was a very bright little girl.'
'Obviously you were right,' Paul Maddox says.
Bridie smiles widely, well pleased.
'Right.' The doctor settles himself and opens the pad on his knee.

'You want me to begin at the beginning, I suppose?' Bridie volunteers.

'That sounds best.'

'I'll have to think for a bit,' Bridie tells the two men, and closes her eyes, already eliminating from her mind the bits she doesn't want them to know.

– Bridie's not in her room, Francis said.

Kathleen shrugged. She's probably gone off by herself. She usually does in the morning. Normally we do get up well before this, she added with a smile.

– Her bed doesn't look slept in.

– Bridie always makes her bed immediately she gets up.

– Oh.

Kathleen poured the coffee and sat down at the opposite end of the kitchen table.

– This is like old times, Francis said.

– Almost.

– Yes. Almost. Kathleen – thanks.

Kathleen gave him a tiny smile and nodded.

– I mean it.

– I know.

– You could have –

– I could have done a lot of things, Francis. I could have tried to be more understanding. I could have tried to help.

– You did try.

Kathleen shook her head. No. I don't think I did. I didn't want to help you, Francis. You know why? Because I loved you so much I was mad with jealousy that you showed Bridie so much love –

– Kathleen –

– I know it was dreadful what you did. I know that. I knew that at the time, but – God. I didn't really give a damn about what was going on between you and Bridie except that she was being given the love I wanted.

– Kathleen –

– Damn you, Francis Lynch. You know I still love you. You know I still need you.

Francis nodded. No more than I need you.

– Do you?

– Of course –

– Do you really, Francis?

– Yes. I do. More than ever.

Kathleen heaved an enormous sigh. I wish I could believe that.

– You can believe it. It's the God's truth.

Kathleen Lynch stared at her husband for several moments, then she reached across the small table for his hand. Holding it, feeling what she could only think of as new energy seeping into her, she asked quietly: The question is, where do we go from here?

– The question is, where do you *want* to go from here?

– The question is, where *can* we go from here?

– The question is –

Suddenly, together, they both laughed, both remembering that spring afternoon in the zoo when Francis had asked her to marry him:

– The question is do *you* want to marry *me*? Kathleen had asked.

– The question is, would I have asked you to if I didn't?

– The question is, are we right for each other?

– The question is, how are we going to find out if we don't give it a try?

– The question is, what happens if we're not?

– The question is, why make problems before they even arise?

– The question is –

And so it had gone, each in turn with a question, and each question in turn getting crazier and crazier, making them laugh uproariously, making the baboons bare their horrible yellow fangs in alarm, sending the capuchin monkeys scampering up the barkless branches that criss-crossed their enclosure, paying no heed to the people who gawked at them in astonishment, their private laughter increasing as they watched those same gawking people crane their necks and look about them in an attempt to discover what was so terribly funny.

– Seriously, Francis, Kathleen said, pouring herself another mug of coffee and passing the jug across the table. Seriously, what do we do?

– When does Bridie start school again?

– I'm sorry? Oh. Two – no, three weeks' time. Why?

– Supposing I stay here with you until after this weekend. Then go back to town until after Bridie has gone to school, Francis said, absentmindedly stirring what remained of his coffee.

– Yes. And then?

– Then supposing I moved down here?

– To stay?

– To stay.

Kathleen smiled. Is that what you want?

– That's what I want.

Everyone in the village had predicted it was going to be a long and very severe winter, and it seemed as though they might be right. Already many of the trees were changing their leaves to gold and orange and glowing brown, and the small birds were hectic, gorging themselves on berries and grubs as if by stuffing themselves now they would survive the treacherous days that approached. The smells in the woods, too, were different: the light, timorous scent of spring had given way to the headier, sweeter perfume of summer and this, now, was on the wane replaced by a pungent, drowsy, slightly intoxicating aroma like that of the lilies which accompanied people to the grave.

Bridie wrinkled her nose and sniffed. For some reason all she could smell was the expensive perfume Mike Petty had brought as a gift for Mummy: paying his way into her bed. And now she had Daddy too.

– Not for much longer, Bridie dear.

– No. Not for much longer.

– Very soon Daddy will be all yours.

– Yes. Very soon Daddy will be all mine.
– And you'll be very happy.
– Yes. We'll be very happy. Happy ever after.
– That's right. Happy ever after like in the stories he used to read you before Mummy sent him away.
– But he's back now.
– Oh yes. He's back all right. But not to you, Bridie. He's only back for Mummy.
– No. I think he's back for me too.
– Why don't you ask him?
– Yes. That's what I'll do. I'll ask him.
– But you'll have to be careful.
– I'll be careful.
– And if –
– And if Mummy is in the way –
– We will –
– Yes.
– And then –
– And then I'll look after Daddy and we'll live happily ever after.
– That's right.

– You'd better tell her, Kathleen suggested, wiping the sink with a rag and rinsing her fingers under the tap.
– If that's what you think's best.
– Yes. It would be better coming from you, Kathleen insisted without really knowing her reason for thinking this.
– You mean in case she hates the idea so she'll blame me, Francis said with a happy laugh. Where does this go? he asked, holding up the pot of marmalade.
– Something like that, Kathleen agreed without laughing. Oh, in the cupboard by the fridge. Top shelf.
– Okay. I'll tell her as soon as she gets home.
– I'll leave the two of you alone.
– Coward.

It would be ever so easy. All she had to do was get Daddy on his own and sit on his lap and put her arms about his neck and cuddle him like she used to and feel him cuddle her and see him smile with his eyes and ask him: Daddy, you did come back because you loved me, didn't you?

And Daddy would answer: Of course, my precious Bridie.

And then she would ask: You do love me much more than you love Mummy, don't you?

And Daddy would answer: Of course I do, Bridie.

And that way it wouldn't matter about Mummy being alive (indeed, it would be better if she was alive since she'd be made to suffer and get put in her place and be taught a lesson for not looking after Daddy properly when she had the chance) because she wouldn't be able to interfere ever again and if she tried Daddy and Bridie would simply pack up and go away together and leave her alone and miserable in her rotten old mill while Daddy took Bridie with him to Egypt and all over the world and showed her all the lovely things and places she had only seen on television or in the magazines that Mummy thought were very fashionable to buy, and all the time he'd love her and cuddle her and make her feel nice and warm.

. . . On the other hand:

Supposing, just supposing Daddy told her that he came back because he loved Mummy as much as he loved Bridie – what then? Well, in that case, of course, Lady would take charge and arrange things. Lady wasn't about to stand by and see poor Daddy share his love with Mummy who slept with Michael Petty and kissed him without caring who saw and wore his stinky perfume and–

And supposing Daddy said he really loved Mummy more than he loved Bridie?

Bridie refused point-blank to think about that. She gazed up into the topmost branches of the huge tree where the owl lived and from where it dispensed its wisdom. Then she stood up, and kissed the tree, running her tongue along the gnarled, rough bark as though seeking nectar, making a curious noise in her throat like humming.

– Where's Daddy? Bridie demanded as soon as she got home,

kicking off her walking-shoes and slipping into her slippers.

– You're late, Kathleen told her, busily making gravy. Daddy? He's in the sitting-room, I think. Why do you ask? she enquired, crumbling an Oxo between her fingers.

Bridie ignored the question and stalked from the kitchen without a word, while Kathleen watched her go and gave a grunt, and muttered 'the cheek of her'.

– Ah, Bridie, Daddy said, turning from the window and looking very handsome in his casual clothes. I've been waiting for you.

– Have you, Daddy?

– Yes. I want to talk to you.

Bridie looked pleased.

– Come in and shut the door.

– *That* sounds *very* serious, Bridie said, shutting the door obediently, and setting her face in mock-serious lines.

Daddy came straight to the point. Bridie, he told her, I'm coming to live with you here.

– Oh, Daddy, Bridie cried in delight, accepting the personal pronoun as singular, and running across the room.

– I'm glad you're pleased.

– It's marvellous, Bridie enthused, reaching up to give Daddy a great big hug.

But Daddy didn't want a great big hug. He caught her by the wrists, gently but firmly, and held her away from him, smiling of course, but holding her away from him nevertheless. I truly am glad that you're pleased. Your Mummy and I were worried you might be upset.

– Mummy knows? Bridie looked puzzled, sounding surprised. Daddy laughed. Of course Mummy knows. We had a long talk this morning and we've decided to try and be happy together again.

– All three of us?

– Yes. All three of us.

– I see, Bridie said, pulling away from Daddy's grasp and turning away.

– Whatever's the matter now, Bridie? A moment ago you were delighted and now –

(All you have to do is ask him, Bridie. Ask him if he still loves you. Ask him if he loves you more than he loves Mummy.)

– Do you still love me, Daddy? Bridie asked without looking at him.

Daddy made a clicking noise with his tongue. What a silly question! he said. Of course I still love you.

– As much as before?

– Every bit as much.

– Do you love Mummy too?

– Yes, Bridie. I love Mummy too, Daddy told her but sounding a bit impatient as if he didn't like all the questions.

But Bridie persisted. Who do you love the most, Mummy or me? Daddy started looking out of the window again. Why all these questions, Bridie? he asked.

– I just want to know.

But Daddy didn't answer that right away. He kept on staring out of the window, his nice big hands hanging by his sides, his shoulders a bit hunched. Bridie moved to him and put one hand in his. I really need to know, Daddy, she told him quietly.

Daddy looked down at her. I love you both the same, he said, giving her hand a friendly squeeze.

Bridie thought about that. And will it all be just like it used to be?

– I hope we'll all be happy, Daddy said.

(That's not what you asked him, Bridie. He's avoiding your question. He doesn't want to answer you, does he?)

– Happy like we used to be? Bridie asked.

– Yes, Daddy said, but he sounded strange, his voice distant as if he was answering a different question.

– Francis? Bridie? Tea's ready, Mummy called from the kitchen.

– We'd better go and eat, Daddy said.

– Will you tuck me in tonight? Bridie asked suddenly.

– Yes. I'll tuck you in tonight if you want.

'Well,' Bridie begins after thinking about it in silence for several minutes, directing her words at Paul Maddox who smiles like Daddy and is much, much cleverer than Doctor Joseph. 'It really became clear that I had to do something after Daddy and I had a long talk,' she says.

Doctor Joseph glances and nods surreptitiously at Paul Maddox who nods back ever so slightly, and asks: 'What was it you talked about, Bridie?'

'I'm coming to that,' Bridie says, putting the two of them in their place, not letting them hurry her, not letting them make her rush into things.

Paul Maddox smiles. 'I'm sorry. Go on.'

'Daddy called me into the sitting-room and told me he wanted to come back and live with me again.'

'Live with you and your mother again,' Doctor Joseph corrects.

Bridie gives him an angry glare. 'That's not what I said,' she snaps. 'And that's not what Daddy said either. He said he wanted to come back and live with *me*,' she reiterates.

'And your mother?'

'She was going to be there too, as long as she didn't start interfering.'

'But she did – interfere?'

'Oh yes. Right from the start.'

'In what way?'

'In every way.'

'Can you give us an example?'

'She kept on butting in when Daddy and I wanted to have secrets.'

'That must have been very annoying,' Paul Maddox suggests sympathetically.

Bridie beams at him. 'It certainly was. *And* she would never leave us alone together. Always snooping and listening.'

'And that really made you angry.'

Bridie nods. 'It made Daddy very angry too, of course.'

'I'm sure it did.'

'Poor Daddy. All he wanted was for us to be happy,' Bridie says wistfully.

'But your mother spoiled all that?'

Bridie nods. 'Yes,' she admits. 'So,' she adds, 'I decided to do something about it.'

'And your Daddy helped you?'

Bridie bursts out laughing. 'Good heavens no. Daddy didn't know anything about what I was planning. I think he'd have tried to stop me. He was very afraid of Mummy, you see.'

'Afraid of her? Why was that?'

'Because when Mummy sent him away the first time she was able to keep me, and Daddy was afraid she might send him away again and still be able to keep me.'

'Oh.'

'And that would have broken his poor heart,' Bridie says, looking ever so forlorn. 'And I couldn't let that happen, could I?'

It was still quite early when Bridie yawned and said she was going to bed.

– Already? Mummy asked.

– Yes.

– You're not sick?

– No. Tired.

– Oh. All right.

– Daddy promised to tuck me in.

– Yes. I'll tuck you in, Bridie.

And Daddy always did as he promised, so when Bridie called down that she was ready he came upstairs and tucked the blankets in, making sure they were secure at the bottom so her feet wouldn't get cold, so the piggies couldn't run to market as he used to tell her. Then, to Bridie's delight, he bent to kiss her good-night. Bridie closed her eyes and puckered her lips. Waiting. Ready to throw her arms about his neck and hold him close to her. But Daddy only brushed her forehead with his mouth, and patted her on the head before switching out the light and leaving the room quickly.

Bridie was stunned. She lay there, staring in silence in the direction of the closed door until she heard Daddy and Mummy talking downstairs. Then she started to scream. She screamed and screamed and screamed.

– Leave her to scream, Francis said.

– What on earth is the matter with –

– Leave her scream, Francis said again.

– What –

Francis gave Kathleen a comforting squeeze. She's angry with me.

– Whatever for, Francis? Kathleen asked, trying desperately to dismiss the awful thought that loomed into her mind.

– For not – she wanted me to – she wanted me to kiss her like I used to, Francis said, looking very vulnerable with his guilt.

– Oh, Francis –

– It's all right. That's over.

– Oh, Francis, Kathleen said again, catching his hand and hanging on to it.

– I was afraid of this. When I was talking to her earlier . . . telling her about my coming back . . . I felt certain she was . . . I don't know how to put it . . . she was expecting me to . . . Oh, Kathleen.

It could have been her husband's mute cry for help, or it could have been that Bridie's screams were getting on her nerves: whichever, Kathleen Lynch left the room and ran up the stairs. She threw open Bridie's door and switched on the light.

– Now that's quite enough out of you, Bridie, she shouted. Stop that screaming at once.

– I want Daddy.

– Well you can't have him.

– I want Daddy.

– He's busy. He's already tucked you in.

– I want him, Bridie wailed.

– You just listen to me, young lady. Daddy and I are busy. One more squeak out of you and I'll give you a thrashing the likes of which you've never had. You just go to sleep and stop being so childish.

– I hate you, Bridie said under her breath.

– What was that?

– I hate you, Bridie hissed, loading her words with venom.

Kathleen gave a scoffing snort. You can hate me as much as you please, young lady. You've had your own way far too long. Just stop that racket and go to sleep. You're nothing but a damn nuisance.

Bridie listened to Mummy going downstairs. It was still too early for Lady to come, but she would come tonight. Bridie was positive of that. She could almost feel her getting ready for the journey from the woods, putting on her lovely silver dress and making herself look pretty. When she arrived they'd settle matters once and for all. They'd show Mummy who had been having her own way far too long. They'd give Mummy a thrashing the likes of which she'd never had. They'd make certain she never came between Daddy and Bridie again. Yes, they certainly would.

– Come and look at this, Francis said.

– Just let me get my nightie on.

– Forget the nightie. Come and look.

Kathleen came to the window and looked. It's beautiful, she whispered.

– 'Shine on, shine on harvest moon,' Francis sang in his awful, unmusical voice, 'up in the sky.'

Kathleen giggled and snuggled close to him. You're *so* romantic. That's the lover's moon. The harvest moon is next month.

– Even better, Francis said. You think the gods lit it specially for us?

– But of course!

– Bless their cotton socks.

Kathleen laughed again. What imagery!

– You know, I don't ever think I've seen a moon like that before.

– You've just never looked before.

– Probably not. Hey, what are those?

– Bats.

– Bats? Ugh. They get in your hair.
– You are a fool, Francis.
– Driven to madness by love.
– What on earth has got into you tonight? Kathleen asked.
– I've never been so happy in my life.
– I do believe you mean that.
– I do. I really do, Francis said. If only . . .
– Ah. I might have guessed there'd be a –
– No. I just thought . . . Francis shook his head.
Kathleen waited, averting her eyes.
– I just thought . . . He stopped again.
– Well, say it for goodness' sake.
– It's a terrible thing to say but I can't wait to get Bridie packed off to school and out of the way.
Kathleen gave a small laugh. Neither can I. What a relief to have someone else put up with her for a change!
– *I* should have been –
– Ssh, Kathleen whispered, putting one finger on Francis's lips.
Suddenly Francis scooped her up in his arms and carried her to bed.

Shine on harvest moon up in the sky, indeed! She certainly had bewitched poor Daddy. Bridie was really annoyed. She sat up in bed, the pillow keeping her upright so that she could see conveniently out of the window. And bats getting in your hair! Bridie had long since discovered that the bats were sent to clear the way for those creatures that preferred the night. Everything was arranged better at night-time: darkness imposed special laws which were scrupulously obeyed. And anything that dared infringe those laws was severely dealt with.
Close to midnight, Bridie leaned sideways and looked at herself in the mirror. She tidied her hair, using her fingers to fluff it out prettily, then settling herself back on the pillow again, waiting patiently.

Ignatious Wyett regarded the bright, moonlit night with a

baleful eye. People scoffed at the power of the full moon, joking about it, fostering scurrilous stories of werewolves and demons. If only they knew! As he, Ignatious Wyett, knew to his cost. Oh, yes, Ignatious Wyett knew all about the malignant forces that roamed the sky when the moon was full, avoiding its brightness and keeping to the shadows, threatening and laden with doom as they were now, this very moment. Ignatious shook his head wearily. It would happen and there was nothing he could do about it. No wonder the images on his wall looked particularly smug. No wonder the grandfather clock in the hall boomed the hour with utter melancholy: *dolente dolore*. And there was nothing he could do. Nothing but wait.

The great bird finally flew across the face of the moon and sent its spirit to Bridie.

– Hello, Bridie, Lady said, standing close to the bed and looking lovelier than ever, her silver dress shimmering, and with flowers in her hair.

– I knew you'd come, Bridie said.

– Yes. I heard you calling me.

– I knew you would.

– Everything will be all right now.

– Oh yes.

– I will guide you and take care of you.

– I know you will.

– You are my child, Bridie. I will always protect you and love you.

And saying that the Lady held out her arms and smiled, and Bridie felt drawn from her bed, felt herself drawn towards the beckoning arms, felt them close about her, embracing her, felt warmth and peace flow into her body.

. . . And Kathleen sat up in bed suddenly.

. . . And Francis asked: What's the matter?

. . . And Kathleen said: I don't know. I'm frozen.

. . . And Francis said: Don't be silly. Cuddle up to me.

. . . And Kathleen said: It's like someone stepped on my grave.

. . . And Francis said: You've been dreaming, that's all.
. . . And in his cottage Ignatious Wyett wept.

– You're sure you'll be all right? Francis asked, standing by his suitcase, jangling his car keys in one hand.

– Of course I will. It's only for a couple of weeks.

– If you need me before that –

– I'll *need* you all right.

– You know what I mean.

– Yes, Francis. Don't worry. I'll be fine.

– Well, I'd better make a move then. Oh, where's Bridie? I'd better not forget to say goodbye to her or you'll have another tantrum to cope with.

– She was here a minute ago. Bridie? Bridie?

Bridie heard Mummy call and took her time about coming to the car.

– Ah. There you are. Daddy's just leaving. Come and give him a kiss goodbye.

Bridie walked towards them, dragging her feet, making them wait.

– Bye, Bridie, Daddy said, leaning down and kissing the top of her head. Bye love, he said to Mummy and put his arms around her and kissed her on the mouth. Then he got into the car, started up the engine and rolled down the window. You look after Mummy for me, won't you, Bridie.

Bridie gave him a smile. Yes. Of course I'll look after Mummy for you.

– And don't give her any trouble.

– No. I'll be very good.

– That's my girl. You'll be in school when I come back, but we'll come and visit you. Anyway, in no time it'll be Christmas and we'll all be together again.

– Yes, Bridie said.

– Mind how you drive, Mummy said.

– I will.

Mummy bent down and kissed Daddy again. I love you, she said.

– I love you too, Daddy said. Bye.

– Bye.

– Bye, Bridie.

– Bye, Daddy.

Daddy waved and waved, steering the car cleverly with one hand, waving and waving till he was out of sight.

– Well, Kathleen said, turning to speak to Bridie.

But Bridie was gone, and was nowhere in sight. Kathleen shrugged and walked into the house, feeling suddenly lonely, but feeling happy too, happier, she thought, than she'd ever been in her life.

'Could I?' Bridie asks again.

Doctor Joseph and his friend and colleaguc Paul Maddox glance at each other. They'd been doing that all morning, giving each other little looks when they thought Bridie wasn't watching, like they were transferring ideas to each other, flashing messages with their eyes. But Bridie had seen them all right.

'Now, could I?' she asks again, keeping them on the hook.

'I can see why you'd think that, Bridie,' Paul Maddox, the ever so clever Paul Maddox, says.

'So, when Lady came to visit me at my request, we decided Mummy had to be sent away.'

'Lady and you?' It is Doctor Joseph's turn to ask.

'That's what I told you ages ago when you first started to question me,' Bridie tells him, her voice scolding. 'And you wrote it down.'

The doctor looks flustered and riffles back through his notes. 'Ah, here it is,' he says, smiling boyishly as if the discovery forgave him his forgetfulness.

'We planned the killings together secretly. That's exactly what I told you.'

'Yes. Indeed you did,' the doctor admits, reading his notes. 'I have it here. That's what you said. Word for word.'

'You see?' Bridie says, pleased as punch.

'So Lady and you planned to – to send Mummy away?'

Bridie nods.

'When was that?'

Bridie frowns and concentrates. 'The night before Daddy went back to the city.'

'So there were three days before –'

'Yes,' Bridie interrupts. 'Lady and I never rush into things. And I needed that time to work out the details.'

'*You* worked out the details?'

'Mostly. But Lady helped, of course. She couldn't be with me *all* the time. She's very busy, you know. But when she came we would talk over my arrangements.'

'And approved them, I take it.'

'Of course. She told me I was very thorough. Painstaking, she called it. "You're very painstaking, Bridie", she said.'

'I'm sure you were.'

'Well, I had to be. It was very important.'

'Yes,' Doctor Joseph says.

Paul Maddox just nods, looking very sad.

'I think we should break there for today,' Doctor Joseph suggests. 'You look tried, Bridie. I know I am.'

'Yes,' Paul Maddox agrees. 'A break would do us all good.'

'As you please,' Bridie says, not feeling in the least tired, but willing for the two men to have a little rest.

'We'll meet again in the morning then.'

'Yes,' says Bridie, getting up and smoothing down her dress.

'It should be our last day for a while.'

'Yes, I suppose it should,' Bridie says, sounding disappointed.

'Bridie?' It is Paul Maddox who speaks, coming to Bridie and putting his hand on her shoulder. 'Do you think you'll be able to tell us all about what happened to your mother tomorrow?'

'Oh yes.'

'You won't find it –'

'Upsetting? No. Not at all. Everyone seems to think I should find it upsetting. I wonder why?'

– You all right?
– Fine.
– Miss me?
– Very much.
– I wanted to call you last night but it was so late when I got home. I thought I might get you out of bed.
– I was up most of the night.
– Why? What happened? Francis asked, sounding alarmed.
– Nothing happened, Kathleen told him. I was just thinking.
– Oh.
– About us.
– What about us?
– About how lucky we are.
– Yes. I'll drink to that. No problems with Bridie?
– No. Not yet anyway. In fact she's being very good. Too good to be true.
– You give her a good smack if she starts playing up.
– She needs a father for that.
– She's got one. Seriously, everything's okay?
– Of course it is, Francis. Don't worry.
– I'll phone you again tomorrow.
– Good.
– Same time?
– Yes.
– Right. Kathleen?
– Hmm?
– I love you.
– I know you do. I love you too.
– Bye.
– Bye.
– Who was that? Bridie wanted to know.
– Daddy.
– I wanted to speak to him.
– I'm sorry. I didn't think. He was in a bit of a hurry.
– He'd have found time to speak to me.
– You can talk to him tomorrow. He's phoning me again.
– I'll answer the phone then.

– If you want. I'm not trying to stop you talking to your father, you know.

Bridie said nothing to that.

– By the way, tomorrow morning I want you to start getting your clothes ready for school.

– I have to go out in the morning.

– Where to?

– Just out.

– Well you can sort out your clothes *before* you go out.

– I won't have time.

– You'll just have to make the time. You're going to have to start behaving yourself now, Bridie. You're far too grown-up to be churlish and sulky.

– I'm not sulky.

– I say you are.

– I'm not.

– Just start behaving yourself, that's all.

She was like a new bride in a new house with new furniture and a new life stretching out in front of her and filled with the promise of love, happiness, and peace. That was what Kathleen Lynch told herself when she got up and opened the curtains and gazed out at the golden, misty morning. She hugged herself, smiling broadly, and did a little waltz about the bedroom, pretending Francis was holding her, swaying her off her feet. She danced to a stop in front of the long, bevelled mirror, and studied herself, not displeased with her reflection. She unlaced her nightdress and let it fall about her feet, adopting a pose reminiscent of that favoured by Hollywood actresses in the forties: one knee bent, buttocks shoved out, an arm raised above her head, the hand limp. Not bad. Not too bad for an old woman! Titty-bags a bit on the floppy side, tummy starting its downward slide, but apart from that, not too bad at all. You're a fool, Kathleen Lynch, Kathleen Lynch told herself aloud, giving her reflection a somewhat bawdy wink. A damn lucky fool.

– Oh. It's only you, Bridie said down the telephone without really thinking. Mummy? It's Granny, for you.

– Hello, mother.

– What did the child mean: only me?

Kathleen tittered. Nothing, mother. We were expecting someone else.

– Oh? Who?

– Francis, Kathleen announced a little smugly and grinned as she heard her mother suck in her breath.

– Francis?

– That's right, mother. We're getting back together again.

– Are you, indeed? Mother sounded almost disappointed.

– Yes we are, indeed.

– I must say that's very generous of Francis.

– Must you?

– I should think it is after the way you treated him.

Kathleen, determined to let nothing spoil her good humour, ignored that. What was it you wanted, mother?

– I hope you realise how fortunate you are, my girl –

– Mother – Kathleen curled the word upwards into a threat.

– Not everyone gets a second bite of the cherry, Mother went on undeterred.

– Mother –

– I just hope you've learned your lesson, that's all.

Kathleen clamped her mouth shut.

The silence, unexpected, daunted Mother. Kathleen?

– Yes, Mother.

– Oh. I thought you'd gone.

– No. I'm here.

– Did you hear what I said?

– Yes. I heard what you said. I'm very fortunate. Francis is very generous. I've learned my lesson. What else did you want?

– Honestly, that grandmother of yours, Kathleen said to Bridie, but in a good-natured way.

Bridie said nothing.

– Right. Now. What have I got to do? Kathleen asked herself out loud. Ah. Your clothes. Have you sorted them out?

– Yes.

– Good girl.

– They're all laid out on my bed.

– You didn't check them for name-tags, did you?

– No.

– Never mind. I'll do that. I'm sure some of the old ones will have come off. I think – I hope – I have a few spare ones, Kathleen said, aware that she was babbling, aware, too, that the word 'name-tag' had settled in her mind, stinging. By the way, she went on, trying to sound casual, do you want to take your new doll with you – the one Michael gave you?

Bridie stared at Mummy. No, she said.

– Where is it, anyway? I haven't seen it since you got it.

For an instant Bridie seemed scared, but only for an instant. In no time she was as nonchalant as ever, even giving a small, apologetic smile before admitting: I'm afraid I lost it.

– Lost it?

– In the woods.

– Oh, Kathleen said, attempting to sound convinced. Why ever didn't you tell me about it?

– I thought you'd be cross.

– We'd better go and look for it then, hadn't we?

– I have looked.

– But if I helped –

– No, Bridie said quickly. No, Mummy. We'll never find it. Anyway, it wasn't really a very nice doll, was it?

– I didn't get much chance to see it.

– Well, it wasn't. And I'm too big for dolls, don't you think?

– Perhaps you are.

– Can I go out now? Bridie asked, already sidling towards the door.

– Hmm? Yes, if you want to. But don't be late home.

Bridie made a face.

– Daddy's phoning.

– Oh yes. I won't be late.

'You're looking very perky this morning, Bridie,' Doctor Joseph points out, not looking all that perky himself.

'I *feel* very perky,' Bridie says, liking the word. 'I've never felt perkier,' she adds.

'Any special reason?'

'Not really,' Bridie says, although well aware there is a special reason.

'Oh.' Doctor Joseph is disappointed.

'Maybe it's because this is our last day,' very clever Paul Maddox says. 'Like getting out of school for holidays.'

Bridie gives him a condescending smile. 'Maybe.'

'Or maybe it has something to do with what you're going to tell us today?'

He *is* clever. 'Maybe,' Bridie admits.

'Oh yes,' Doctor Joseph puts in, *trying* to be clever by pretending he has forgotten what was on the agenda. 'You are going to tell us all about how you and Lady – how did you put it? – how you and Lady sent Mummy away – that was it, wasn't it?'

Bridie gives him a look that dubs him a fool.

Paul Maddox rescues him. 'I'm sure Bridie remembers exactly what she said.'

'Indeed I do. Every word.'

'You see?' Paul Maddox asks Doctor Joseph who doesn't answer, looking chastened.

Then the two men wait for Bridie to tell them all about it, and Bridie makes them wait a little longer than need be, enjoying their rapt attention, looking forward to leading them up the garden path. 'Well,' she says finally, 'to begin with, Daddy telephoned like he said he would. And *I* answered the phone.'

'Was that important? That *you* answered the phone, I mean?'

'Very important. I had to be sure Daddy wanted me to send Mummy away, didn't I?'

'And did he?'

'Of course he did.'

'He told you that?'

'Yes,' Bridie says firmly, and watches the two men start passing looks again.

'What exactly did he say, Bridie?'

'He said it was a brilliant idea,' Bridie tells them.

– Oh. Hello, Bridie. How are you?

– Very well, thank you, Daddy.

– Good. All ready for school?

– Nearly.

– It won't be long now.

– No.

– Is Mummy there?

Bridie scowled. She's in the garden. She'll be in in a minute.

– Oh.

– Do you miss me, Daddy?

– Yes. Of course I miss you and Mummy.

– Me, Bridie insisted. Do you miss me?

Daddy sighed. I said I did, Bridie. Get Mummy for me, will you, like a good girl.

– She's coming. I can see her coming, Bridie lied.

Daddy started to whistle through his teeth.

– Daddy?

– Yes, Bridie?

– I've had a brilliant idea.

– Have you? What's that?

– Well, it's like a game.

– A game. I see.

– A pretend game.

– I see. And what do we pretend?

Bridie took a deep breath. We pretend Mummy's gone away and that there's just you and me.

– Oh brilliant, Daddy said, sounding very cross. Bridie, stop being stupid and get Mummy for me this instant.

– But Daddy –

– Is that Daddy? Mummy asked, coming into the hall.

– No, Bridie snapped, and slammed down the phone.

But Daddy rang back almost immediately and he and

Mummy had a long talk, laughing and joking together, and Mummy saying 'She never said that? The little vixen!' and 'Of course I miss you, darling' and 'I love you too' and then putting down the phone and standing over it, touching it with her fingers as if she was touching Daddy's cheek like she had done when he visited, her eyes all soft and doting.

– I hear you told Daddy you wanted to pretend I'd gone away, she said to Bridie later.

– It was going to be a game.

– Well, you'll have to think up another one. I don't know what's got into you, Bridie. I would have thought you'd be pleased we were going to be a family again.

But Bridie wasn't pleased. She was hurt by Daddy's rebuff, and livid that he had told Mummy.

Overnight the weather changed. It was a dismal morning, grey and dark and teeming with rain. Great clouds plunged upwards across the sky presaging a thunderous storm. The world, alas, is tombal, Ignatious Wyett told himself, and all men shudder at the prospect of imminent death. He shuddered. Life's ineluctable bailiff gallops in to claim the tattered remnants of the soul before it disintegrates. Ignatious sighed. No sign of a friendly God, no guiding angel. Only death's lowly rasophor to gather up the pieces and scatter them at the feet of an uncaring Christ. Perhaps to be banished to eternal hell. Ignatious shook his head sadly. Still, there was, as Blake well knew, a path through hell, which was a good thing. It offered hope, and while there was hope there was –

Abruptly Ignatious Wyett became alert, frowning, listening. But not for any sound, it seemed. It was as though he had heard something whispered in his brain, had just missed catching it, and was waiting for it to be repeated. And soon, out of the blue, it came again. Sacrifice! The single, frightening word filled his consciousness. Sacrifice. The pacification of demons. Ignatious shot out of bed and hurried, still naked, downstairs.

– What ghastly weather for your last day at home, Mummy said.

– It's right, Bridie said.
– Right? What's right about it?
Bridie shrugged.
– She doesn't know, does she, Bridie?
– No, she doesn't know.
– But we know.
– Yes. We know.
– Soon.
– Yes. Soon.
– I will help you.
– I know you will.
– Don't be afraid.
– I'm not afraid.
– You're very quiet, Mummy said.
– Just thinking, Bridie answered.
– What about? Mummy wanted to know, trying to be jolly.
– This and that.
– Looking forward to school?
– Oh yes.
– Good. It *will* be nice for you to have other girls to play with.
– Very nice.
(You're weird, Bridie Lynch, Patricia Brazier said in a loud voice. That's why no one wants to play with you.
I'm not, Bridie said.
Yes you are. Even the teachers think you're weird.
They do not.)
– And then there's Christmas to look forward to.
– Yes.
Mummy reached over and patted her on the head. Cheer up, for goodness' sake.
– I'm quite happy, thank you.
– You could have fooled me.
– Oh, we've fooled her all right.
– Yes we have, haven't we.
– Will you just wash up these few things while I make my bed? Mummy wanted to know.
– Yes.

– Thank you.

Humpty Dumpty sat on the wall, Bridie said to herself as she washed up those few things. Humpty Dumpty had a great fall, she said as she put the few things away in their proper places. Silly Humpty Dumpty should have known better, she thought, as she took the wide, pointed knife from the drawer and tested its sharpness with her finger. He shouldn't have been on the wall in the first place. He shouldn't have been where he wasn't wanted. Causing trouble. Interfering.

Bridie took the knife with her when she went to the foot of the stairs, listening to Mummy singing 'Shine on, shine on harvest moon' as she made her bed.

'That's not what your father told the police, Bridie.'

'I know. The Inspector told me.'

'He said – your Daddy – he said he told you to stop being stupid.'

Bridie smiles her most sorrowful smile. 'Poor Daddy. He's always forgetting what he says. I even heard Mummy tell him he'd forget his head if it wasn't screwed on tight.' Bridie laughs gaily at that. 'Don't you think that's funny?'

If they do, neither of them laugh.

– Anyway,' Bridie continues, paying no heed to the silence. 'Anyway, *I* knew what Daddy wanted, so I went ahead with my plan.'

'To kill your mother?'

Bridie nods yes.

'Can we just stop there a minute, Bridie?' Paul Maddox asks, clearing his throat with a short cough. 'What I'm really interested in are the feelings you had during all this. Just before you killed your Mummy, what were you feeling?'

Bridie looks puzzled. 'I never thought about *that* before,' she admits.

'I'm sure you felt something. Were you frightened, or nervous, or did you feel guilty?'

Bridie sucks through her teeth. 'I know I felt excited,' she confesses.

'Nothing else?'

Bridie shakes her head. 'Nothing I can think of at the moment.'

'Didn't you feel sorry for your mother?'

'No . . . well, maybe a bit *after* she was dead, when she was lying there looking up at me all hurt and bewildered. I think I felt a bit sorry for her then.'

'And since you've been here?' clever Paul Maddox continues to probe, waving a hand that seemed to embrace the whole, huge, redbrick hospital. 'Since you've been here, have you thought about what you did at all?'

'Sometimes. Sometimes.'

'And how do you feel about it now?'

Bridie cocks her head. 'Just the same,' she says. Then she leans forward. 'I'm going to tell you a secret,' she announces, smiling to herself as both men lean forward too, their eyes brightening with expectation. 'Sometimes at night when I can't sleep, I feel I *want* to be sorry,' she tells them. 'But then that feeling goes away and I feel nothing at all.'

What was it he had told Bridie on that fateful day when she had tripped up his path like a maiden sweet carrying her treacherous innocence in both hands like a deadly posy? 'There are far worse things than death, you know', he had said. And now Ignatious Wyett knew, by premonition or foreglimpse or prescience or through some divine knowledge bestowed by a faltering angel, that death was at hand. And it was not creeping stealthily up on him as one might imagine: it howled about him, blustering its way to his mind, slapping him on the shoulder like some old familiar.

Standing there, naked, looking absurd, looking pathetic, looking abandoned, looking grotesque, the small, empty phial still in his hand, eyes bright, shoulders squared and head thrown back in that attitude of mystical resignation appropriated by martyrs and fools, Ignatious waited for his extravagant sacrifice to be resolved. He had so little time; so very little time. Already, he knew, the dour forces of calamity were mustering their daemonic weaponry, swooping in on the child, requisitioning her mind. So very little time.

– Mummy, Mummy, Bridie called. Come quickly.

Mummy came to the top of the stairs. What is it *now*, Bridie?

– It's Daddy. On the phone. Something terrible has happened.

– Oh my God, Mummy exclaimed and came down the stairs very quickly.

– Now, Bridie. Now.

As Mummy reached the bottom step and made for the telephone, Bridie stuck out her foot and tripped her, sending her sprawling on the floor, scudding a little way across its polished surface. At what seemed a sedate pace under the circumstances Bridie walked over to Mummy and stood over her as she tried to get up. Then, with Mummy on all fours, Bridie plunged the knife into her back between her shoulder-blades.

Ignatious Wyett screamed for death to come. Shadows clustered over him, laughing and mocking his futility. He felt life shiver from him with extraordinary precision, and all the while his mind filled with a booming voice, crying, 'Too late, too late, too late.' A face, wide and white and lined, peered at him, mouthing soundlessly, but somehow conveying the melancholy message that his sacrifice had been a waste of time.

Bridie watches Mummy die, studying the unedifying process of death. Oddly, Mummy didn't look frightened, or even angry. She looked, it seemed to Bridie, puzzled; and when she gurgled and the trickle of blood seeped from her mouth, there was nothing but bewilderment in her eyes.

'You know you will have to say here for some time, Bridie?' Doctor Joseph asks, closing his notebook, and putting the top on his pen before returning it to his top pocket.

'Oh yes,' Bridie says cheerfully.

'You don't mind that?'

'No. It's quite nice here really. And Daddy can always come to see me, can't he?'

'Yes, he can come and see you,' Doctor Joseph tells her, his voice suggesting that he didn't think Daddy *would* come, which Bridie has guessed anyway.

Poor Daddy, Bridie thinks, closing her eyes and seeing Daddy being helped from the mill by two big strong men who almost had to carry him. Poor Daddy. Still, he'd come to see it her way when the time was ready. 'He won't come yet, of course,' Bridie says. 'He'll have to think things out, won't he?'

Paul Maddox nods and says: 'Yes, I suspect he will.'

Later, alone, waiting for the pretty, coloured tablets, the nurse had given her, to take effect, Bridie sits on the narrow metal cot and gazes about the little room. It is very nice and neat. Everything clean and tidy and in its proper place: the small table and the chair cleverly screwed to the floor to make sure they stay neat and in their proper place. She feels pleasantly drowsy and lies back, watching the daytime grow old and grey through the window set high in the far wall, thinking how thoughtful someone has been to set it that high, that close to the sky where the great owl flew. Peacefully she closes her eyes, her pretty eyes, her eyes like fabulous emeralds, as someone once told her.